KIRAKEE'S WOLF PACK
(HOWL UPON THE MOON)

BY
KC Morcom

Reviewed by Emma Megan for Readers' Favorite

Kirakee's Wolf Pack: Howl Upon the Moon by KC Morcom is a remarkable young adult fantasy with an anti-bullying theme.

I can't remember when I last read such a wonderful, sad, and moving story with so many twists and turns packed with mystery, action, and adventure. This irresistible mystery fantasy about a divided kingdom and different worlds that unexpectedly connect is well worth reading.

I made a wish to meet a black panther,
and it came true!

In loving memory of
Tarbu, the black panther.

Published by KCM Inspirations,
Launceston, Tasmania, Australia.
ABN: 97 095 689 033

Kirakee's Wolf Pack (Howl Upon the Moon) by KC Morcom.
Cover Design and Cover Artwork by KC Morcom.
Author/Story, created by KC Morcom. Illustrated by KC Morcom.

This is a work of fiction.
Names, characters, places, and incidents either are the product of the author's imagination or are used fictitiously. Any resemblance to actual persons, living or dead, events, or locales is entirely coincidental.

PUBLISHER NOTE

Although the information in this book is believed to be accurate at the time of going to press, neither the author nor publisher can accept any legal responsibility or liability for any errors or omissions that may have been made.

ISBN: 978-0-6489164-7-5
ISBN: 978-0-6489164-8-2
ISBN: 978-0-6489164-9-9
ISBN: 978-0-6454889-0-6

A catalogue record for this book is available from the National Library of Australia

Table of Contents

Table of Contents

Howl Upon the Moon

Chapter

1

It's the last day of the third-year senior high school final semester. The classroom is laced with the scent of stale lead pencils.

Thirty students race to finish the final term's project for the chance to win a scholarship for a subject of their choice for the New Year.

The class teacher, Ms. Time, stands up and addresses the class. 'Come on, students, only one hour to go,' she says as she claps her hands.

Kira quickly focuses her eyes back down on her work. At this point, she is working on her final illustration and paragraph for her project. Out of all the students in the classroom, she has been the most determined competitor to win the scholarship.

1

Ms. Time slowly tours the classroom, stopping at each student's desk to enquire about what subject they have chosen. She reaches Kira's desk and gently removes Kira's slightly matted, long dark brown hair from draping around her face.

'This looks interesting. What is your subject about, Kira?' asks Ms. Time.

Kira silently spreads the stack of pages over her desk for Ms. Time to see. Kira does not speak much in class. In fact, she has not spoken much at all since her mother went missing several months ago.

Ms. Time slides her hands over the paperwork. 'I see, Wolves,' she smiles. 'That is an intriguing subject to cover. Well done, Kira.'

Ms. Time does not say anything else, but she knows Kira's choice of subject is for her to follow in her mother's footsteps since her mother was an environmentalist and conservationist for wolves.

Ms. Time begins to walk away but steps back to Kira's desk and quietly says, 'Would you please see me after class. I have something to give to you.'
Kira nods in agreement.

Ms. Time has taken a shine to Kira and is concerned for her welfare. She wants to help her in any way she can as a teacher.

Prior to Kira becoming a new student at the school, she was moved around into multiple foster care homes after her mother disappeared. It was a few months before her less-than-caring aunt, Kira's mother's sister, reluctantly took on guardianship of Kira.
For this to happen, Kira's aunt had to return from an overseas trip, and she was not at all impressed with the forced change of plans. Kira had to relocate to her aunt's hometown.

It has now been four months at the new school, and the new school transition has not gone smoothly either. A few of the students have made Kira a target for bullying.
She is smaller than the senior student of her year, and she has not spoken much since arriving. The less than empathetic students are adding to her grief by frequently causing problems and trouble for her.

All Kira wants to do is find out what has happened to her mother. Her mother was also her best friend, and now she feels like she has nothing left to make her feel safe and happy.

Most recently, the authorities have upgraded Kira's missing mother status to the status of assumed dead, but Kira does not accept this status since no one has ever found a trace of foul play or evidence of her being deceased.
In fact, Kira suspects deception because there are things she knows, yet others claim they do not know, but Kira believes someone did know about what she was doing when she went missing. Her mother had communicated with her coworker about her work in the field. Even Kira had seen her doing homework on her computer with filling out field reports. Besides, she had told her some stories of her findings, and since, all records of her work have disappeared like they never existed.

For now, Kira's biggest goal is to win the scholarship and be able to choose environmental studies with the hope that this will be a steppingstone for her to get into the same career as her mother. Her plan is to go out into the field as soon as possible if her mother is never found. She strongly believes there is something suspicious about her disappearance.

So far, her wolf project has been easy to do. A great deal of the information in the project is what her mother had told her. However, since the project involves telling a story too, she has been able to create illustrations from her own dreams, but these visions in her dreams seem to be so very personal, and she would often wonder if they were related to her wish, her own personal situation, or inspired by her mother's love for the wolves.

The dreams feel more real than familiar. Sometimes she has been able to smell the breath of a young wolf puppy and feel its loneliness and sadness. Some of the dreams have shown the pup happily playing with another pup.

One night, just before Kira went to sleep, she made a desperate plea to the powers of the universe for her mother to be found and for better things to come, and that included being surrounded by people who loved and cared about her. That night she had a dream that the young wolf was wishing and making the same plea by howling upon the moon.

The next day, Kira figured it was her own mind creating dreams that were of her own life experiences. But the one thing that has bothered her the most is the sense of how the surroundings in her dreams seem so real.

A forest filled with tall trees is something her mother told her about in one of the locations she had been investigating, where the wolves were becoming ill and even some dying. Kira's mother had befriended one she-wolf expecting pups, but upon birthing, only one of the pups had survived out of the litter, due to which Kira's mother suspected they had died from being exposed to something in the environment.

Before Kira's mother's disappearance, Kira never had a bother in the world. The only thing she ever wished for was to be able to meet a black panther someday. But believing that was too much of a big wish, she settled for wishing for a statue of a black panther when her mother told her she was returning from a field trip with a big surprise for her.

Kira's mum sounded excited, and Kira was hopeful of a wishful outcome.
However, the surprise gift was not what Kira had hoped for, and neither was her reaction what her mother had hoped to see. The gift was a black and white striped skirt with a matching scarf.

Kira's mother had thought Kira would be pleased with her gift since she had taken a shine to decorate her bedroom with black and white, as well as being a big fan of black and white photos.

Ever since that day, Kira has never been able to forget the disappointment on her mother's face. She knew there was something missing to Kira's reaction. Kira often goes over the moment—the memory.

'What were you hoping for, my sweet girl? I can tell you are disappointed,' Kira's mother asked.

Kira leaned over and gave her mother a hug. 'Sorry, mum. It's just me. I do like my present. Thank you.'

Kira's mum leaned back and looked at Kira in the face. 'But there is something else. What is it? Please tell me. I know you must have been thinking of something else.'

'It's okay, mum. I'm just being silly, and I've been wishing for something that is impossible, and you would never have guessed what it is because I've never told you.'

Her mother put her hands on her shoulders, crouched down to her face, and looked her in the eyes. 'Please tell me what it is. I will understand. I haven't been able to give you much over the past few years, but if I know what it is you really wish for, I will save up and one day buy it for you.'

Kira smiled and gave her mother a big hug. 'You're the best mum. I will tell you, but one part of it will surely be impossible but the other possible.' Kira cleared her throat. 'Well, I've always wished to meet a black panther.'

Her mother's eyes lit up.

Kira continued. 'But I know that is impossible, but, if possible, I would love to have a black panther statue one day.'

Kira's mother sighed with relief, then gently chuckled. 'Well, I'm glad to hear that. I can do a statue, but as for meeting one, even I would love to do that one day too, but I think we will settle for a beautiful big statue too with one that really looks like the real size black panther. We can buy from one of those fancy big boutique shops, and we can put it in a special part of the house where it can take pride of place, so we both can enjoy it. What do you say?' she said with a smile.

Kira hugged her mother again and thanked her.

Although it has been several months since that conversation, no matter what, even though the mystery of her reaction was resolved, Kira has always been haunted by the vision of her mother's disappointment on that day, and it has saddened her.

That matching skirt and scarf have been one of the only possessions Kira has of her mother now since moving away from her hometown, and it had been the one thing she had worn often since her mother's disappearance until she began the new school.

On the first day at the new school, she wore the skirt and scarf, but unfortunately, it drew the attention of the bullies. They teased her about her outfit by calling her Zebra until no one felt comfortable enough to talk to her in fear of the bullies picking on them too.
Ever since that day, she has not worn the outfit and has now wrapped the scarf and skirt in tissue paper and put it away in a safe place in her wardrobe.

Plagued by memories, she now feels the need to unravel the mystery of her mother's disappearance. The last thing Kira knew about what her mother was doing was the day she went missing. She was heading out on a field trip to the untouched location she had chosen not to publicly reveal for the sake of protecting the wolves.

Something about Kira's dreams has consistently been bothering her, though. She still feels the elements in her dreams as feeling real. The warmth of the sun on her face, the scent of the forest trees, and visions of a running river into a lake that shimmers with the reflection of the moon, and in the distance, she can hear the faint howl of a wolf. The images, the sensations, the scent, the sounds linger as if she is there. Not all seems sweet and charming, though. In fact, the forest has a sense of gloom; something dark and evil lingers. Most often, she has been awoken from those parts of the dreams, leaving her feeling fearful.

Kira looks back over her shoulder and sees Ms. Time strolling down towards the back of the classroom but catches

the stares of the class bullies sitting behind her. The look on their faces is all too familiar to Kira. They stare with an evil smirk, almost as if they are targeting their prey for dinner.
Kira swiftly avoids further eye contact with them, turns back to her desk, and begins getting back to work.

Suddenly, her chair and desk jolt forward. Her lead pencil streaks up over her illustration, and the rest of her project pages fall off the desk and scatter all over the floor.

One of the bullies sitting directly behind her has just kicked Kira's chair with the force to push her forward.

The leader of the bullies who they call, Snake, because everything she says is like venom coming out of the mouth of a snake, taunts Kira.
'Woof, woof, Kira. Teacher's pet,' she sarcastically snigger's.
Kira ignores her and proceeds to collect the pages from the floor and quickly sits back down at her desk and begins rubbing out the pencil line over her illustration.
Shortly after, she returns to the very last paragraph of her story, but before she can finish it, the school bell rings.

She puts her face in her hands and feels defeated. Today was her only chance to submit her project. Tears begin to well up in her eyes.

Kira walks over to Ms. Time's desk once everyone has left the classroom.

Ms. Time opens her desk drawer and takes out of the drawer a brand-new hairbrush.
'This is what I wanted to give you. We have a few in supply in the school aid room. I think this will help since your aunt hasn't bought you a new brush as requested.'

Kira reaches into her school bag, then pulls out a hairbrush along with an envelope from her aunt, addressed to Ms. Time.

'Oh, I see! Your aunt has already taken care of that matter as requested, but haven't you used the brush yet, Kira?'

'Yes, Miss Time.'

Kira gestures for Ms. Time to open the envelope.
Kira's aunt has provided a small note. Ms. Time frowns as she reads.

'Well, I see. Your aunt has told me she has acted on my suggestion of providing you with a new hairbrush and says she has bought you this one with bristles made from pig's hair. I think she meant to say Boar's hair instead?'

'I'm not sure, Ms. Time. She told me it's pigs' hair too.'

Ms. Time senses the sarcasm in Kira's aunts' note as she also expressed, she did not appreciate being told what to do by teachers and considers it rude manners.

Ms. Time knows the brush with Boar's hair is not sufficient for Kira's long thick hair, and that would explain why her hair is still partly matted.

'I'll tell you what we will do, Kira. I'll give you this brush as an extra in case you would like to use another with your new one. There is no need to tell anyone about your gift. Are you okay with that?'

Kira nods in agreement.

Ms. Time picks up Kira's project off her desk. 'What's happened here, Kira. You haven't finished?'

Kira's eyes well up with tears; her heart is sinking. 'No, Ms. Time. There was an accident with the pencil, and I used up most of my time for removing the pencil streak and repairing the image.'

Ms. Time gently puts her hand on Kira's shoulder. 'Do not worry. There is a simple solution for this. You can finish it up at home tonight, and I will drop by your home tomorrow afternoon to pick it up. How does that sound to you?'

Kira's face lights up. Her face beams with a bright smile. She nods in agreement.

Finally, some peace. The project can be submitted on time with the help of Ms. Time, and at last, some time out from the reckless tactics of the school bullies will be a relief.

Ms. Time walks Kira out to the main front entrance of the school. 'Don't worry, Kira; I will see you tomorrow.'

Kira walks down the steps onto the parking lot, turns around, smiles, and then waves goodbye to Ms. Time.

She looks up towards the sky. There is a storm brewing. Her hair flies up and down in the strong wind exposing her matted hair knots at the nape of her neck.

Ms. Time calls out, 'Hurry home, Kira. It looks like it's going to be a big storm.'

Kira quickly sets off towards home. She clings to her project in her arms, holding tightly so the wind won't catch the paperwork.

One minute's walk outside of the school, she captures a glimpse of Snake with her friends in a street lane-way.

'Hey Kira, what's you got there,' Snake bellows.

Kira steps up her pace even more, hoping to put a good distance between her and the bullies. However, Snake and her company are relentless in their pursuit like a pack of wild Hyenas.

They gain ground on Kira and are now on her heels.

Kira looks back over her shoulder to check their distance from her.

Snake puts her hand on Kira's shoulder, brings Kira to a complete stop, and forces Kira to turn around and face her.

'Trying to avoid us, are you Kira?'

Kira attempts to walk away, but Snake grabs her again. She grabs Kira's paperwork by snatching it out of Kira's arms.

'Now, what have we got here? All about wolf wolfs,' she laughs.

Kira attempts to regain her paperwork back off Snake, but Snake is relentless and won't let go.

'Come on, Kira! Be polite and ask me politely to return your project.'

But without Kira being able to reply in time, Snake has other plans.

With the flick of the wrist, Snake lets Kira's paperwork fly off into the wind.

Kira leaps up into the air to grab the papers, and for the first time, she protests with a blood-curdling scream, 'NO!'

As Kira's feet begin to return to the ground, Snake shoves Kira, pushing her back. Kira loses balance and crashes to the ground. Her head bounces twice on the pavement and completely knocks her unconscious.

One of the group of girls quickly attends to Kira. She taps her on the face. 'Kira, are you okay? Please wake up!'

Snake looks on in silence. She looks worried.

The girl holding Kira on the ground looks up to everyone and yells, 'Quick, go and get Ms. Time. We need an ambulance. Kira is bleeding. Go!'

Everyone, except for Snake, runs back to the school. Ms. Time is just beginning to get in her car. The girls' bodies tremble with fear as they tell Ms. Time about what has happened.

12

Ms. Time sharply yells, 'Quickly, get in the car.'

They arrive down the street where Kira's motionless body lays on the pavement. Snake kneels over her body and has laid her jacket over Kira to keep her warm.

Ms. Time quickly attempts to wake Kira up before she calls for an ambulance.
Within minutes the ambulance and the police arrive.

Kira begins to gain consciousness, but all she can feel is the warmth of Ms. Time holding her hand.

Finally in the hospital, the medical staff rush around attending to her. The room is filled with the sound of machines and doctors giving orders to nurses.

'Quickly! Get the life support machine. We are going to lose her. Her brain is swelling too much. We need to intubate her right now. Stat!'

Kira begins to hear the machines and voices fade away. A dense darkness starts to become her world. A sense of confusion looms. Just as all becomes black and silent, a small pin of light breaks through the darkness, then slowly grows bigger and brighter. In the distance is a voice.

> 'Be strong, Kira. Wake up!'
>
> The voice sounds like her mother's.
>
> 'Is that you, mother?'
>
> The voice gently replies, 'Be strong, my sweet girl. I'll be with you. Now wake up.'
>
> 'Where will you be with me?'
>
> 'Drink the water of Orphaned River,' the voice instructs her.
>
> 'What do you mean, mother?'

As the light slowly begins to fade away, the fading voice replies, 'Not here, but I won't be too far away.'

Kira yells out, 'Mother, please don't go! Please don't leave me.'

Just as the light slowly came and went, a golden glow replaces the darkness.

'Mother, please don't go! Please don't leave me,' Kira repeatedly calls out.

But in the golden glow, another voice replaces her mother's.

'Wake up, sleepyhead; you're dreaming.'

The twinkling sunlight beams through the trees, it blinds all vision. She sits up, tries to refocus, and constantly blinks. She looks around, then has eye contact with a critter friend.

For a moment, there is an eerie kind of silence while attempting to comprehend what is real and what is not.

'Who am I? I'm not Kira? Mother was calling me Kira.'

A raccoon laughs. 'No! You're Kirakee of Morakee. You've been dreaming.'

Kirakee leaps up and looks at her tail and legs. 'I dreamt I had no fur, and I heard mother speaking to me.'

'It was only a dream, Kirakee. You were calling out to your mother again in your sleep. Come on, sleepyhead, we must get you back to your home den before your aunt growls.'

The Forbidden

Chapter

2

Upon arrival back at her home den, her greeting from her aunt is of the usual criticism.

'Kirakee, you must stop being friendly with the forest animals. It brings shame to the Wolves. I forbid you to see them any longer.'

Kirakee does not want to shame the wolves, but she feels the request from her aunt to refrain from her new friendships will be difficult to fulfill since days with her forest critter friends have been her best days. They make her feel like something significant. Life with her forest friends makes her life feel like it is something meaningful.

Prior to her friendship with the forest critters, her life looked very different. The only thing that remains the same is her surroundings.

Blessed is the land, dominated by tall pencil pine trees. Surrounding the forest lays an abundance of water. On one side of the forest flows the 'Orphaned River,' which runs into the 'Two Moon Lake.' Both the river and lake divide the land.

On the far north side of the Orphaned River, Kirakee's wolf pack made their home den in a small cave. Surrounding their den are several other wolf clans, and some of them are related and well known to their territory. Many of these packs work together to protect their home area from danger by guarding their territory boundaries.

Kirakee's wolf pack had several members. Originally there was her mother, now presumed deceased. Her mother had been exiled from another land with her sister, but before her mother was exiled, she gave birth to three pups but only brought two of her pups with her to Morakee.

Once her mother settled in Morakee, she gave birth to Kirakee. But not long after Kirakee's birth, her mother disappeared. It has always been presumed her disappearance took place during a wolf pack patrol mission, but no one has ever been able to find any evidence of her deceased body.

Kirakee's aunt eventually became her sole carer, taking over her mother's role, but before she settled into her new role, she disappeared for a brief time. Upon her return, she gave birth to another pup from her union with Kirakee's father.

From her mother's first litter of pups, Kirakee has two brothers, much older than her, and a sister she has never met since she stayed back with her own father in her mother's old territory. Kirakee's brothers regularly patrolled and guarded the surrounding land until most recently.

There was a time when she enjoyed the company of her new sister from her father and aunts' union.
Her new sister spent many days frolicking around with her in the nearby forest.

However, her friendship with her sister was shortly lived when Kirakee's aunt privately received news from one of the Legends pack members with secret information. The information was sensitive, and no one else was meant to know of the news other than who the Legends member chose to tell.
The Legends pack are the wisest wolves of the forest. They know about everything before all other wolves learn about it.

However, upon the news being delivered, Kirakee's sister Morana secretly overheard.
'One of the daughters of your den will become a leader when she is at her greatest strength. She will bring change to the Kingdom of the wolves,' he whispered.
Although Kirakee was aware her sister had overheard the conversation between the Legends member and her aunt, Morana changed and began to exclude Kirakee by not revealing what she had heard.
'It's for me to know, and you will never need to find out.'

From that day forward, Kirakee's and Morana's loving relationship changed for the worst. Even her aunt began to treat Kirakee with much less care. What Kirakee does not know is that her aunt and Morana are determined to make sure that she will never be capable of becoming a leader; they believe Morana should be the one to rule the kingdom of the wolves.

Ever since that day, they have given Kirakee tasks beyond her skill set and strength, which has only caused her to fail, lose her confidence, and not feel strong enough to become a leader.

She has grown to become a very shy wolf. She was always the smallest for her age but is beginning to look like the smallest of the pack.

The only thing she holds close to her heart now are the memories of her mother. The memories included her mother telling her to embrace her difference.

But it has been difficult to do when her sister Morana calls her 'Witches Poo.' A name Kirakee hates because not long before she began calling her the name 'Witches poo,' Morana claimed there was a rumour about a witch in the forest who was becoming known for taking the spirit of the wolves for herself. This act would leave the wolves wandering around without their souls until they die a brief time later.

Morana considers Kirakee to be the rejected waste of the witch, and this really upsets Kirakee.

Feeling lonely and confused, she attempts to make a change.

'Auntie, would you mind if I venture out into another part of the woods since you don't want me hanging around with the kind of friends I've made?'

Her aunt straightens up and nods, 'Yes, but I warn you. You must never drink the water of the Orphaned River, or you will become lost. Nor must you venture around the Two Moon Lake after dark, as danger lurks in those parts.'

Kirakee wags her tail and nods, 'I promise, Aunty; I'll be careful.'

Off she goes with a little more confidence in her stride as the excitement for a new adventure spurs her on.

She approaches the boundaries of the Orphaned River. She recalls her aunt's warning not to drink from the river, but her curiosity gets the better of her. She wonders what is wrong with the water.

Gradually, inch by inch, she moves closer to the river until she is standing at the edge of the riverbank. She watches and listens to the rumbling of the rushing water.

'It looks normal to me,' she whispers.

Behind her is rustling and loud cracking within the trees. She looks back over her shoulder. There is an eerie kind of darkness slowly moving towards her. It isn't like anything she has ever seen. Nothing like a storm. This darkness radiates intense heat, and she has an intense sense she is not alone.

She quickly turns around and bellows, 'Who is there?'

The darkness is beginning to look like thick smoke. There is a powerful force in the darkness. It begins pushing her backward, and with not being able to see anything clearly, she is unaware of exactly where to put her footing to avoid falling off the riverbank.

She struggles to fight back, but every move she makes just inches her closer to the edge.

Suddenly, she loses footing and slips down the edge of the riverbank.

Half of her body emerges into the river. She can feel the force of the river's current grabbing her. She clings to the edge and fights to hold on.

Then, as quickly as when she fell into the river, a glittering shine begins to emit from the water. She feels an unexpected sensation of comfort. The water feels soft and calming. Within seconds, something below pushes her up out of the water.

She grabs the top of the riverbank and finally can pull herself up to safety.

The glittering glow follows her. It illuminates in the darkness. There is a soft, gentle, and warm breeze surrounding her, and it gently laps around her ears.

She gasps! She looks up and looks around. There is the smell of wild blossoms, her mother's favourite scent.

Feeling warmed and comforted, she gently wags her tail, then whispers, 'Mother?'

With an ear-piercing scream that makes Kirakee cringe, the darkness quickly moves away. Kirakee is bewildered about what has just happened. The twinkling light has disappeared too.

Trying to shake off the sensation of confusion, she shakes her fur coat to dry, takes a deep breath, and gathers her thoughts once again. The experience has left her with many questions and triggers more memories of her mother.

She shakes her head, *'No, don't be silly. Of course, she wasn't here.'*

She recalls an instruction her mother gave her.
'Never go into the water. You must not do this, ever! It is not safe for you. Clean your fur coat by rolling around in wild blossoms.'

Kirakee has always remembered her mother's instructions, and up until this very day, she never knew what it would feel like to be submerged in water. It was not what she imaged, and now nothing makes sense.
The only conclusion she can come to is her lack of experience and knowledge about this new boundary is why these things have surprised her to be strange, weird, and frightening.

'I really need to get out of here,' she mumbles.

So, without another moment of hesitation, she hastily speeds off towards the Two Moon Lake.

Very quickly, she arrives at the lake. It looks amazing. Fish are jumping in and out of the water. The sun is reflecting off the lake. The twinkling light looks like bright stars. There is a soft breeze blowing over the water, creating glittering ripples on the surface of the lake. It is calm. She feels a sense of peace.

She begins exploring the surrounding area, but time begins to rush away, and it is becoming late.

She senses an urgency to leave; she must not be there after dark.

As she begins to leave and head home, she is surprised by another wolf. He is friendly.

Kirakee is charmed by his appearance. He is strong.

They sit together for a while. Her friend does most of the talking. He tells his back story about how he comes from another wolf pack in a territory on the south side of the Two Moon Lake and usually comes to the lake to hunt during the day.

While she intently listens to his story, she begins to become quite fond of him and instantly grows a little crush.

He seems to be fond of her too. 'Will you come back and see me here tomorrow?' he asks her.

Kirakee nods in agreement. 'Yes! I'll come back for sure.' She is thrilled she has met a new friend.

He offers to walk her out of the surrounding forest of the lake as time has slipped away.

It is close to dusk, but as they are leaving, they walk into trouble. Not too far ahead, there is a pack of rebel wolves.

'This is bad,' her friend says.

He can tell this pack is very territorial, and they will not let them pass without making it difficult.

Suddenly, the leader of the pack jumps out in front of them. He is big, angry, and fierce.

'Fools, why do you tread here?'

Frozen and trembling, Kirakee bravely replies, 'Sorry! We don't want any trouble. Please just let us pass, and we will be on our way.'

Then without another word spoken, the rogue leader grabs little Kirakee and throws her up against a large tree. She hits the tree with great force.

Her friend is angered and reacts. He leaps onto the rebel wolf and courageously battles until the rogue wolf retreats.

Although Kirakee's friend wins the battle, he is injured. Kirakee swiftly gathers him to his feet, and they quickly retreat.

Finally, they are out of harm's way, but he is not in good shape. Kirakee attends to his wounds and looks at him admirably for being her hero. She now feels affectionately close to him.

The very next day, Kirakee keeps her promise and heads back to the lake to meet her new friend. Not far into her journey, she meets another she-wolf from one of her territory clans and invites her to join her on her reunion with her wolf friend.

Unfortunately, when Kirakee's newfound friend meets Kirakee's newest company, instantly, they take a shine to each other.

This is an awkward moment for her; it is making her feel like she is in the wrong place at the wrong time. But they are older and stronger than her, so she feels she must accept the fact they would end up liking each other more than just friends like she is to them.

After a long day of adventures, Kirakee's friends ask her to come back to meet at the lake again.

She straightens up, wags her tail, and nods, 'Yes! That would be great, as long as we don't have to encounter any more crazy wolves.'

Her he-wolf friend assures her not to worry. 'I know of a safe place where they won't find us.'

The next day, they climb rocks while roaming around the lake banks, laughing, and playing. Kirakee embraces every moment. However, the sun is beginning to set.

Kirakee requests they leave now.

'Please, don't leave yet,' her he-wolf friend insists. 'I've found a safe place where we can hang out for much longer. It will be safe, even if it becomes dark.'

'Please, Kirakee. Let's stay longer,' Kirakee's she-wolf friend pleads.

'Well, if you really must then, but just for a little while longer,' Kirakee replies.

They enter a small cave, but Kirakee does not think the cave looks very secure. It looks more like a gap in between the rocks.

The moon is full, and the moonlight is reflecting off the lake, projecting the appearance of two moons, making everything look lighter and brighter. It has become much later than what it appears to be.

In the distance is the faint sound of a howling wolf. This sound bothers Kirakee. She almost feels like the howl is calling her, and along with the concern about the late hour, it is beginning to feel like a really bad day.

'We really must go now. You can always see each other again tomorrow.'

Her friends agree to finally leave.

Just as they begin to step outside the cave entrance, they hear rustling in the nearby bushes.

'Quickly hide,' Kirakee nervously whispers.

They huddle back down into the deepest and darkest part of the cave.

Suddenly, the light dims, and there before them, blocking the light, is a big dark figure of a wolf.

Shocked, they 'gulp' and 'gasp.'

'You again,' growls the rogue wolf. 'Did you not learn your lesson before?'

Another voice shouts out, 'You shouldn't have come back.'

Kirakee clears her throat, 'We are leaving now—' Her voice cuts off with a dry squeaky sound.

She takes a deep breath, trying to expand her diaphragm so she can make herself appear bigger.

The crazy wolf pack laughs.

Kirakee straightens up again and takes another deep breath. 'We are leaving now. We don't want any more trouble.'

Kirakee and her friends stand on their feet and move forward toward the entrance.

'Oh no, you don't. You're not going anywhere,' growls the

leading rogue wolf. 'Especially you, Kirakee, you're not going anywhere at all.'

Kirakee gasps. 'How do you know my name?'

'You are to come with us,' the rogue wolf growls.

'Where? I'm not going anywhere with you,' she growls. 'I don't even know who you are and what you want with me.'

'Well, little one, my name is Saber. I think your friends should go, and you stay right here.'

'No! Let her go!' growls Kirakee's he-wolf friend.

Saber angrily snaps, 'Would you prefer to leave your other she-wolf friend with us then?'

Kirakee's he-wolf friend lunges forward. 'Leave them both alone.'

Kirakee whispers, 'Run!'

They all run for the cave opening. Kirakee's friends quickly make it outside, but Saber and his pack members grab Kirakee and bring her down.
She struggles and fights back.

Just as she sees a small opening between her and the pack, she dashes to the opening of the cave.
In amongst all the confusion and darkness, the pack does not even get to see her escape.

Finally, she is free. She runs for her life.
Her friends are nowhere to be found. They have disappeared.

Feeling hurt, bruised, alone, and abandoned, she musters up the strength to make her way home.

As she is passing three Water Rats, she hears them laughing at her, 'Ha, ha, ha, What's wrong with you?'

'I've been attacked by crazy Saber and his crazy wolf pack,' she sobs.

'Yeah, yeah, sure. As if that really happened,' says one of the rats.

She feels ridiculed and humiliated.

'Not even them horrible things care to take me seriously,' she murmurs while limping away.

Her next concern is arriving home so late. The fear of her aunt's furious temper—she just cannot deal with. If she knows where she has been, she could only imagine her aunt not even being a little bit empathetic.

Therefore, she makes a promise to herself to never tell her aunt and family of what has happened for fear of being ostracised.

'Where have you been, and why are you home so late?' snaps her aunt.

Kirakee trembles, fearing her aunt will be able to notice something is wrong.

'Sorry, Aunty, I didn't realize it was so late because of the full moon.'

Her aunt is annoyed. 'Go to bed, you annoying she-wolf,' she snaps.

Kirakee puts her head down and slowly walks away. She is relieved she has not been punished any further.

Kirakee never saw her two friends ever again, and the only thing she ever heard was news that her territory clan friend had moved out of the territory of Morakee.

Since that day, sadness has loomed about her lost friendships. They never came looking for her to see if she was okay, and that has severely bothered her.

She begins to be very withdrawn and does not go out into the forest anymore. Each day, she only steps outside her family den to do the duties her aunt orders her to do, but every other moment she spends a great deal of the time sleeping. That is the only thing she feels like doing right now.

She often sees in her dreams the strange beasts and wolves she has dreamt about many times. They do not make her feel threatened even though she does not know who they are. She has even wished for them to be a part of her life when she has made a desperate plea for her mother and brothers' return, and for change when she has howled upon the moon.

Hush

Chapter

3

Winter came and passed. Spring is now in the air.
It is Kirakee's favourite time of the year. Everything has come alive again. The birds are chirping. All creatures are roaming about, happily making their nests and new homes and gathering extra food for the arrival of their new babies. The butterflies are dancing in the air, while flowers are beginning to bloom everywhere.

Inspired by the beauty of her surroundings and the warmth of the sun, she begins to feel a growing motivation to explore new parts of the woods.

It has been a long time since she spent any time with her forest friends in the woods, since her aunt has disapproved of her friendship with them.

However, her little friends still visit her often by hiding in the trees outside her family den.

After her terrible experience at the Two Moon Lake, Kirakee musters up enough courage to return to the lake, but upon her sister Morana hearing of Kirakee's pending trip, she insists she should join Kirakee.

Kirakee is hesitant to take Morana with her, as she is feeling cautious about dealing with any trouble that might arise with Morana's presence, but she gives Morana the benefit of the doubt.

Upon the sister's arrival at the lake, Morana sights a bear drinking water on the opposite side. Morana fears the bear and begins freaking out, yelping, and howling.

Kirakee runs over to her sister and attempts to calm Morana down.

Kirakee snaps, 'Hush! you're going to attract us a lot of trouble.'

Morana becomes more stressed, and the only thing Kirakee can do is grab her sister by the scruff of her neck and drag her back into the woods.

Just as her sister begins to calm down, and without warning, there is a massive loud noise piercing the air. The noise is so loud it causes their ears to ring.

Kirakee shouts, 'There is danger! Run Morana.'

In pursuit are two human hunters with guns.

Bullets closely fly over Kirakee and Morana's heads.
As they run past the trees, bullets splatter the wood.

This human encounter is something they have never seen before, but they recall the stories told by the wise wolves. The wolves were to fear man as man feared the wolves.

Kirakee's thoughts turn to her brothers since they have gone missing during a wolf pack patrol, and she wonders if their disappearance has anything to do with these humans.

Kirakee and Morana eventually escape from their dangerous encounter with man, but Kirakee fears Morana will make trouble for her if she reports what happened at the lake. So, she asks Morana not to tell, but Morana holds it against Kirakee and uses their secret as blackmail, forcing Kirakee to slave for her on a greater scale than ever before.

As home life does not get any better and more responsibilities are being bestowed upon her, she does what she can to avoid her home life by staying in the woods more often.

One of her little forest critter friends, Tuck, the raccoon, makes an appearance while Kirakee is out scouting for food.

They are thrilled to see each other. Tuck wants to help Kirakee in any way he can and offers to provide her with a meal.

Tuck arrives back about 10 minutes later with a feast of food. Kirakee questions him about how he obtained the meal so quickly.

He admits he has stolen it from some wolves who had buried it. Tuck believes the wolves will not miss it, but Kirakee is nervous and tells him to return it right away before the wolves' return.

But before they can even begin to take the stolen goods back, one of the owners of the food arrives.
The wolf is angered by theft. Kirakee attempts to persuade the wolf that it was an honest mistake and informs the wolf she was about to return the food when she discovered it belonged to someone else.
The angered wolf is not convinced and threatens to tell Kirakee's family about what he believes she has done.
Kirakee pleads with him not to tell her family, but he insists he is going to pay her family a visit.

Kirakee runs home. She is dreading her family being told of what has happened, but she also knows how her aunt will react if she does not tell her first. Her aunt hates being told about bad things that happen with family members through others.

Just as she arrives home, so does her aunt at the same time.
Fearing her reaction, she briefly waits, letting her aunt rest, before breaking the bad news to her.

Nervously, she approaches her, hoping she will be calm.

'Aunty, I have something I have to tell you. I'm sorry if it upsets you, but...' Her voice nervously squeaks and cracks. She clears her throat. 'I want to tell you before you get told by someone else. Another wolf is coming to see you today or tomorrow.'

She begins to explain everything to her aunt, but before she has a chance to finish telling her everything, her aunt boils up with rage. 'How can you do this to me. I've just got home after working all day to bring us something to eat, and the first thing you do is come in and anger me with this problem.'

Kirakee feels sick; she can feel the vomit at the back of her throat. She gulps, then takes a deep breath. 'I'm so sorry, Aunty.'

'Saying you're sorry isn't good enough,' her aunt growls and then lashes out at Kirakee by driving her back into the deepest and darkest part of the den.

Her aunt continues to growl, 'You were told not to hang around with those forest creatures. I'll say it again. You are not to see any of them ever again, or you'll be sorry.'

Meanwhile, in the present, she is regretting of ever telling her aunt about what happened because no one ever came to her home to tell.

Nine days later, while hiding in the den, recovering from the shocking encounter bestowed upon her by her aunt, one of the wise wolves of the 'Legend Pack' comes calling.

'Are you Kirakee?'

'Yes!' she curiously replies.

'Is your aunt home?'

'No, she has gone hunting.'

'Okay. Well, maybe you could answer a few questions for me. I have been told by one of the forest creatures that there has been a great deal of trouble in your home, and no one has seen you for nine days. Why would this be so?'

These questions trouble Kirakee. She does not feel safe telling the wise wolf the truth for fear of her aunt's anger. She fears more trouble.

She begins thinking of what she could say.

Should I say a bunch of trees fell on me? A massive rockfall came crashing down on me. I had a herd of bison run over me. Hmm, it sure does feel like any one of those things did happen, but I've never heard of any wolf ever living after such things happening. I've got it; I'll say this.

'I'm okay. I had an accident and sustained an injury while falling down the side of a hilltop. I then rolled and landed into a big thorny thistle bush, and then a large rock landed on top of me.'

The wise wolf looks stunned and stares in silence for a moment before he speaks.

'Shocking!' He shakes his head in disbelief. 'Well, I'm glad to know you survived all of that, but if you ever have any other problem and need any help, please come, and see me!'

'Okay, thank you,' she smiles.

As the wise wolf walks away, Kirakee takes a deep breath and exhales a big sigh of relief. She appreciates the wise wolf offering to help and the fact he showed he cared, but she is so relieved he believed her even though she told him a lie. But that is all she feels she can do right now to protect herself from her aunt, as she also fears her aunt will drive her out of her home den if she has any other reason to be displeased with her.

Later that day, her aunt arrives home. She tells her why the wise wolf came to Morakee and explains what excuse she told him. Kirakee's aunt stares at her in silence for a moment, then nods her head. 'Okay, that's fine.' She then walks away.

At that moment, Kirakee feels she has made the right decision not to tell the wise wolf the truth.

Relieved she has not upset her aunt; she hopes this will be a reason for her aunt to stop harming her.

33

It has been a few months now since her brother Dasher went missing during a territory perimeter pack patrol. Her other brother, Conan, has not been seen either after he went looking for their brother Dasher.

Dasher was always strong, and when home, he protected Kirakee from her aunt.

No one really knows what happened to Dasher, but it is suspected that he drank some contaminated water which caused him to become ill, lose balance and become injured from a fall, and he was taken away by a human. This has been a problem for a few months, and now they are hearing about the increased presence of man.

Dasher had previously warned them of more humans entering the woods nearby, more than ever before.

Dasher reported, *'The humans don't seem to be hunting for food, but they have been threatening many of the wolf packs by chasing all wolves away from their hunting grounds, and even worse, many wolves have been shot dead.'*

None of the wolves understand why the humans are invading their territories. They especially do not understand why the humans are destroying members of the wolf packs since none of the wolves have threatened the humans. This event is creating an increased fear amongst the wolves, causing the packs to split up and leave behind their sick and old.

This news is worrying for Kirakee and her family. This problem has been affecting the packs by restricting where they can now make their dens. These threats are beginning to affect their strength and survival.

When they were asked what the packs should do, Conan was adamant they all stand their ground. *'Never leave. This is our home, and it's all we have ever known. We don't want war and should do our best to show man we only want to live in peace.'*

Dasher did not agree; he had other ideas. *'Peace? What is that now?'* He growled. *'If they cause us any harm, we will have no choice but to fight back. We will protect ourselves and our home.'*

A new patrol pack member has arrived with the latest news.
He warns, 'Stay away from the Two Moon Lake. This area is mostly affected. The humans have only been in the woods in the daylight. So, the lake is now not safe day or night.'

'Hmm, don't I know it,' Kirakee whispers to herself. She looks up at her sister Morana and shakes her head, jesting not to speak of their earlier ordeal.

Morana replies with an agreeing nod.

Kirakee retreats to the family den. Stricken with sadness, she lays motionless. The news of more lives being lost and still no sign of Dasher and Conan is all too much to deal with.
She knows there will not be much time left to look for them before the winter season arrives again. The snowfall is just going to make it impossible to pick up their scent trail.
She can only hope her brothers will be able to return safely.

Eventually, a few more months pass, and her patience has run short. The snow has set in, and there is still no word of Dasher or Conan. She feels useless not being able to help in any way. They are constantly on her mind.

With the lack of gathering of food supplies and constantly running low, the pack is growing tired and weak. She is concerned for the health and well-being of her family.

Nightfall arrives with a full Moon. She can see the hilltops clearly from her den. Night-time feels much safer than daylight right now because of the presence of man.

Everywhere around looks so quiet and peaceful, and there is no sense of any kind of threat nearby.

Tempted by the calm, she makes her way to the hilltops. Climbing up the hill is not so easy with the thick snow coverage.

Finally, she is at the highest point. She stands there in awe, looking out over the hills, woods, and valley, but something catches her attention as well. In the far distance, there is a strange green glow coming from the snow.

'What is that?' she whispers. 'I've never seen anything like that on the ground but only in the sky.'

Although she is curious and would head down the hills to investigate, she fears it is not a safe option to do right now with all the elements as they would not work in her favour.

She settles to thinking about her dreams—her wishes. The things that give her comfort and hope.

All things have become incredibly quiet on the home front, even more so than the previous winter. Fear runs through the wolf packs. As for Kirakee, there is a greater calm with her aunt since she avoids her quite often.

The Gathering of the Wolves

Chapter
4

The snow is finally melting, and as usual, the forest is coming back to life. This spring is to be even more special.

Every few seasons, there is a gathering of the wolves, and this season the packs are to gather in the Morakee territory. This big event motivates everyone. They all begin planning for the arrivals. There is much work to be done.

The freezing cold months have strained the pack's food supply. Many wolves have starved and become weak, so there is a greater need for more activity to collect sufficient stores of food.

Kirakee is extremely excited about the gathering of the wolves. This will be the first one she will attend.

She finds a spot of blossoms down by the stream. These are the same blossoms her mother favoured.

Kirakee plans to coat her fur with them for the big event. But first, she has a list of duties to attend to around her home den.

'One more chore, and then it's time to clean up,' she whispers.

'Hoot! Hoot! A voice appears from behind her.

She swiftly turns around. It is Tick Tock and Tuck.

'Oh no! What are you doing here? Quickly, come inside and hide,' says Kirakee.

She rushes them into the dullness of the den.

Tuck places his hands on his head. 'Sorry! Don't want to be causing a panic. Just thought we would come by and wish you well for tonight's wolf gathering.'

'Well, thank you, Tick Tock and Tuck, but you must leave. There will be trouble if my family finds you here,' she says with a look of panic.

Just as she warns her friends, she hears a humming sound coming from outside the den. She turns around and walks outside.

'Oh, no! A nest of wasps is attacking everything.'

She frantically runs around in circles. 'What am I going to do?'

Still concerned about Tuck and Tick Tock's presence, she runs back into the den.

'You must go right now. Please hurry! I'm going to be dead when my aunt finds out.'

Covering the food was her very last duty, but being distracted by Tuck and Tick Tock, she had not been fast enough to cover the supply before the sunlight would attract the wasps to it.

Without a word, Tuck and Tick Tock hurry away.

Kirakee frantically digs around, trying to cover the supply hoping the wasps would go away, but it is not working.

Fearing her aunt's wrath, she can only think about finding her father and telling him first in the hope that he will protect her from her aunt.

She runs as fast as she can through the woods, calling out for her father.
Along the way, not far ahead of her, there is another wolf in the woods, so she runs over to him.

'Do you know where my father is?'

'Is there a problem, Kirakee?' he asks.

Kirakee explains what has happened and asks him to tell her father if he sees him to urgently come home.

Her search for her father has used up precious time. It has become late. She needs to head back to Morakee and try to solve the problem once again, hoping that her father will turn up in time.

She arrives back at her family den and continues digging away. She is becoming very dirty and stressed.

'This is like a nightmare. Wish it would all go away,' she murmurs.

She pants and gasps for air. Wasps sting her on the nose. Dirt gets in her eyes.

'Kirakee, you foolish she-wolf, what have you done?'

Kirakee leaps up and turns around with fright upon hearing her aunt's voice.

She looks up at her aunt. 'I'm so sorry, Aunty. I'm trying to clean up the problem. I'm trying to fix it.'

Her aunt had received the bad news from a wolf in the woods about Kirakee trying to find her father and why.
Angered by the news, she came straight home to see this for herself.

'Trying to fix it? You stupid she-wolf. Look at what you've done,' her aunt angrily shouts.

Kirakee pleads with her aunt, 'I'm so sorry, Aunty. It was an accidental mistake.'

Her aunt aggressively stomps on the ground. 'You're sorry, you say? Sorry, you'll be.'

She leaps toward Kirakee, snarling and growling. Kirakee races into the den to avoid her. Her aunt chases until she ceases her.

When she finally stops snapping and growling at Kirakee, she walks away from the den.

She stops, turns back, and instructs Kirakee, 'When I get back, you better be gone from here. I want you to leave after tonight and not come back. Now I'll have to go out and find more supplies, all because of you!'

Kirakee sits for a moment in silence. She is shocked about all that has gone wrong. She cannot believe she couldn't even be saved again by her father from her aunt.

She now begins to cry; she whimpers and howls.

Feeling lost about what to do next, she still tries to dig the dirt around the food store to rid the wasps, but it has become very late, and the gathering of the wolves is drawing near.

Feeling dirty and stressed, she heads on down to the stream to roll nearby in the blossom patch, hoping to remove some of the dirt off her coat.

Not too far away in the distance, she can hear the howls of the wolves. It is time; the guests are arriving.

Instead of joining the gathering straight away, she watches from the dense forest.
The wolves look excited—a big contrast to how she feels right now. This is not how she expected to feel during the biggest event of her life.

After a short while, she musters up some courage to join the guests. She moves in slowly, but when she gets closer to the wolves, she freezes.

In her head, she hears her aunts' words. *'When I get back, you better be gone from here. I want you to leave after tonight and not come back.'*

Feeling sad, worried, and self-conscious, she decides to huddle down below a nearby rock, allowing her to watch everyone from a distance.

'I don't belong here. They are all having a good time. They look happy,' she whispers to the rock beside her since she doesn't have anyone to talk to about how she feels.

As the night goes on into the late hours, the wolves begin to go home to their dens. She has nowhere to go; therefore, she heads off into the woods.

'Hey Kirakee, over here!' a voice loudly whispers.

Tuck and Tick Tock had been watching the gathering of the wolves from the treetops. She tells them about what happened after they had left her home.

Tuck and Kirakee walk together through the woods for hours while Tick Tock flutters from the treetop branches, looking out for any kind of danger.

'What am I going to do? I have nowhere to go,' she sadly says.

Tuck gently puts his hand on Kirakee to comfort her. 'You go home. Things will get better tomorrow. You can't stay out here alone. I must go home too.'

Tuck speaks consolingly with sincerity. 'I'm sorry this has happened to you, and I wish I could help by taking you home, but I think my parents will have a heart attack if I turn up home with a stranger, especially a wolf.'

She decides to risk it and act on Tuck's advice.

As she nervously approaches her home den entrance, she sits outside for a while, staring. It is cold, and she begins to shiver.

Slowly and quietly, she crawls into the den, being careful not to wake anyone.

Once she reaches the deepest and darkest corner of the den, she lays down feeling exhausted and quickly falls to sleep.

The next morning, she awakes to her aunt walking away from where she lay. Without a word said, her aunt has placed some fresh eggs in front of her for breakfast.

As it turns out, word had traveled around about what Kirakee had done, so the wolves at the gathering brought a huge pile of supplies and gave it all to her family. There was more food than her family had ever had before at any one time.

She is relieved. Some good had come out of a really bad day for once.

Soon after, a spark of excitement for her family wolf pack has arrived. Her distant sister 'Cloud' has given birth to a beautiful pup.

Kirakee's sister Cloud who is from her mother's first litter of pups has come to live with the pack for a while, and for the very first time, this is Kirakee's opportunity to get to know Cloud since Cloud, for most of her life, has only ever lived with her mother's first family pack.

Kirakee spends a great deal of time helping Cloud out with her new pup and makes a conscious effort to make sure the little family is safe and well. Cloud is troubled, though, and seems to be quite sad at times.

'What made you come here to Morakee?' Kirakee asks.

'I had to and didn't have too many other choices, but I don't talk about why because Aunty said it would be best to not have everyone know.'

Kirakee sits next to Cloud. 'You can tell me, though?'

'Yes!' Cloud nods. 'I had to leave my pack because it didn't feel safe there anymore. The father of my pup left me. He chose to return to his old wolf pack. I had to fend for myself. It was too hard, so I had to come here to be safe. So here I am!'

Kirakee places her head on Cloud's shoulder to comfort her. 'I'm so sorry you've been through that. We will always take care of you.' She then straightens up. 'Did they chase you away?'

Cloud shakes her head. 'No, they didn't. I made a healthy choice to leave.'

'Well, you know, Cloud. I will always be here to take care of the two of you.'

A few weeks pass. Cloud is still feeling troubled about the abandonment of her partner. She longs to return to her own wolf pack. She misses her home. Her pup has grown bigger and a lot stronger.

When all the family packs are gathered at the den, Cloud feels this would be the right time to announce her departure for her to return to her home.

'I love you all, but I need to go. It is time for me to return home. I would really like to thank you all for having me. Thank you for your care and kindness,' she says with a quiver in her voice.
'I'm sorry I'm leaving right now, but I will come back and visit, and when I have my own den, I hope you will want to visit me too?'

Kirakee is saddened by the news but feels she should support her sister's decision. 'Yes! Yes! for sure. I'll come and visit both of you as often as I can. We all will, right?' Kirakee looks around at everyone else.

Everyone is saddened and bothered by their departure, especially Kirakee. She will miss their company.

Kirakee's aunt and father have become very upset about Cloud's departure. They have grown rather close to Cloud's pup.

'How can she just leave us like that and take away that little one. That little she-wolf loves her poppy. This has upset your father very much,' Kirakee's aunt says to her.

'This worries me too, aunty, but we can always find a way to visit them.'

Her aunt angrily shakes her head. 'Sure, but it's not going to be the same. I think she is very selfish to take her pup away from all of us.'

Kirakee feels she shouldn't disagree with her aunt but wonders in some way if there is reason to be concerned.

Shortly after, Cloud departs from the Morakee territory, but Kirakee keeps her promise to visit her. She makes a journey to see Cloud and her pup again, and this becomes a regular thing for her to do. She does not tell Cloud about the feelings of the family and only wants to do what she can to support her.

Cloud's pup is growing bigger and stronger, but Kirakee is seeing things that are of concern. She sees that Cloud is displaying the same kind of aggressive temper towards her own offspring as she has experienced with her own aunt. This begins to make her reflect on her own life, making her feel very depressed.

A couple of days later, Cloud bellows out to Kirakee. 'Why don't you get up and do something instead of just sitting around here?'

Kirakee begins whimpering. Cloud quickly moves to calm her down, but Kirakee just feels like a worthless burden.

Cloud takes her down to the stream for a drink of water. She sits close to her. 'This is our aunt's fault. She has made you like this.'

She was right. The constant belittling has affected Kirakee, but there were so many other things that have been wrong that Kirakee does not tell Cloud about. Bullying, abandonment, exclusion, and ridicule have made her fearful and sad.

Kirakee whimpers uncontrollably. She finds it difficult to stop until she becomes too tired and falls asleep.

Not feeling comfortable being there any longer, she decides to leave and go home.

From that moment on, she just cannot shake that constant sad and anxious feeling.

Storytelling Time

Chapter

5

Eventually, after being home, she becomes friends with another she-wolf named 'Chip' and spends a lot of time at Chip's own den.

'Kirakee, we should go out more often. I've been hearing about a storyteller down by the border of the Orphaned River.' Kirakee's droopy ear pricks up, and she nods her head in agreement. 'Yes! This sounds like what I need.'

Chip leads the way in the direction of the river.

As they approach, Kirakee can see ahead of her a big, dark, and quite striking he-wolf with a shiny coat. She is bedazzled by his appearance.

'Is he the storyteller?' she asks Chip.

'Yes! And the best one around, I'm told,' Chip says with a smile.

Kirakee is beginning to feel excited. She can tell there is something special about this wolf. Something about him looks familiar, though, and she is curious as to why.

'Welcome to Storytime, my fellow she-wolves,' says the storyteller.

'Hello, I'm Chip, and this is Kirakee from the Morakee territory.'

With a smooth and gentle voice, he replies, 'Nice to meet you. So glad you could make it to my Storytime gathering.'

Kirakee is a little lost for words. She stares in silence while Chip finds a comfortable spot to sit.

'So Kirakee, the shy little she-wolf, and Chip of Morakee, my name is Mon Stark, but you can call me Stark for short. Please sit down, and I'll tell you, my story.'

Kirakee thinks about how he is a magnificent and mysterious wolf and cannot wait to learn more about him.

They sit quietly and listen intently to Stark's story. His back story is about another land—a land unknown to Kirakee and Chip.

'I originally come from the 'Land Warriors' wolf pack.
'Our pack once lived far, far away on the outer edges of the forest. We are the oldest wolf pack of the land and ruled the land for many new eclipses of the Sun.

'My wolf pack only bore pups with the darkest shades of fur. Only very few ever grew to have a slightly lighter shade, but they all still were darker than any other pack of wolves in the forest.

'For many seasons, the land was plenty, and we were the greatest hunters of the land. We also lived in peace, and if any of our pack became divided, we never fought with them and never bore war against any other wolves.

'However, many seasons ago, man began to invade the land nearby, making homes for themselves. They feared our presence, so they began destroying members of my pack, and taking away our pups.

'We never knew what war meant until man came and began killing and taking our own away from our families. We fought back, but the humans were powerful with their guns.

'All the pups were either raised by man and then gradually introduced into the more common wolf packs in far distant forests. Some of the more common wolf packs had also been raised by man and relocated into unknown forests.

'I've been traveling everywhere to find these wolves who are of my bloodline in the hope of teaching them about their heritage. Many I have found have embraced their roots, with some of them returning to the Land Warriors to find their parents. The others who have the knowledge now have their

own gathering of the wolves so they can share their heritage and pass what they have on to their offspring.

'Only a few of my original pack still exist, but a much smaller number than we used to be. We now live deeper in the forest but have been exiled from our original land and ways of life.

'My wolf pack needs to stick together so we can keep our culture alive, the Land Warriors culture, but my pack often suffers from illnesses and famine now.

'Many times, I have met new wolf packs, or they have invited me to come to their pack and share my story, but not one of them has invited me to permanently live with them.

'Not long ago, I was invited to a wolf pack of another origin upon them hearing about what I do. They were keen to learn about my species of wolves and invited me to stay, but once I arrived and they gained knowledge of my breed, they sent me away because, as they said, 'Right type of animal, but wrong kind of breed.' They were afraid that if they accepted me into their pack, then other wolves of my type would be attracted to their pack and feared this would attract man.

'Ever since, I haven't given up, and I continue to travel and tell my story. Although some won't accept me or my story, there are more who already know but don't want to talk about it. However , since man has been moving further into the forests, and because of the many threats, they are eventually going to have to appreciate and understand the message in my story.

'Lessons are learned from past experiences. These are the things that might break you, but they also can make you grow stronger too. The outcome depends on how you embrace them.'

Kirakee is amazed and in awe. *'Wow, this wolf knows what he is talking about. I hope I can get to know him better and learn more about him,'* she contemplates.

She stands up and wags her tail. 'Thank you for sharing your story with us. So much tragedy. We should all accept each other's differences,' she says. 'When I arrive home, I'll definitely be telling my family of your story,' she wags her tail and smiles.

Kirakee and Chip return to Chip's den, but the very next day, Kirakee heads back down to the same place where they had met Stark. She is hoping to see him again and hopes to get to know him much better, but once she arrives, she cannot see him anywhere.

'Maybe he has moved on to another territory?' she whispers.

Dreams; Friends or Foe

Chapter
6

Feeling disappointed she has not found Stark; she tries again to find him the very next day.

Not far into her journey, she hears the voices of her forest critter friends and sees them running towards her.

'Kirakee, we have been looking for you everywhere.'

They all look extremely excited, jumping up and down while circling around her.

'We have some exciting news for you. We met a wolf named Mon Stark, and he is looking for you. He asks a lot of questions about you,' Tick Tock says.

Kirakee's heart leaps with excitement. 'Where did you see him?'

'He was actually crossing the boundary to the Orphaned River,' says Tuck.

'Hmm, are you sure he was going into the Orphaned River? It's not safe to go there,' she says.

'Yes, yes! He didn't seem to be worried about the river,' says the little squirrel named Squeak.

'Okay, thank you for letting me know, my little friends. I think

I shall wait until early tomorrow to find him.'

Early the next day, without a moment to spare, she sprints off from her home down to the Orphaned River. As she approaches the boundary, she stops and stares at the surrounding. She hesitates to move forward. The feeling of her experience here still feels so intense.

Courageously, she takes a few steps forward, takes a big breath, and then another few steps forward.

'Ha, this isn't too bad; nothing feels unusual,' she whispers.

Feeling a little more assured that all seems safe, she walks closer to the river's edge.

A few steps in front of her is a fallen tree. It looks as if the tree has been lying on the ground for an exceptionally long time. Moss covers the entire area of the trunk. It is close to the riverbank and looks like a safe spot to sit while she looks out for Stark.

It has become late in the day, and she is losing hope of seeing him again. Feeling disappointed, her mood becomes low, and it makes her feel weary.

Rather than giving up entirely, she has a plan.
'This is a good spot. I'll just stay here and rest,' she whispers.

In a small area below the tree trunk, she digs up the soil and digs at the brittle log to make a small den—a place she will be able to feel safe to sleep.

She quickly drifts into a slumber and once again dreams of the strange beasts. The visions in her dream seem so very real, almost as if being there at the Orphaned River; she is watching them.

In her slumber, she hears a voice.

'Kirakee, Kirakee...Wake up,' whispers a gentle voice.

Gradually she opens her eyes.

'Kirakee, wake up, you sleepyhead,' the voice whispers again.

Am I dreaming that voice? She asks herself while still trying to open her eyes.

'It's me, Stark.'

She tries to focus, and gradually as her vision begins to clear, she sees Stark sitting before her.

She gasps. 'Stark!' she says with excitement.

'Don't be afraid, but...'

Before Stark finishes what he is saying, she senses they are not alone. There is a large shadow blanketing her.

She feels there is something behind her. She looks up.

'Gasp.'

Her heart leaps, and she begins to tremble.

'Yes, I was trying to tell you before you noticed,' Stark says with a smile.

Over to her right is another figure moving towards her. She blinks and blinks, believing she needs to clear her eyes and refocus.

'Am I still dreaming?' she asks.

'No, this isn't a dream,' Stark smiles. 'Meet Tarkin and Sheena,' he chuckles.

Above her head, standing over the fallen tree trunk, stands a black panther, Tarkin, and walking towards them with a slow plod is a golden lioness, Sheena.

Not being able to believe her eyes, she shakes her head and continues to blink.

She stands to her feet and steps forward out of her little den.

'Oh, I get it. I'm still asleep. It's a dream,' she chuckles with an upright tilt of her head.

Convinced it is just a dream, she relaxes, yawns, and stretches.

'Okay, guys. What's on the menu for today. What kind of adventures are we getting up to today in my dream?' she says with a snub tone in her voice.

Stark moves forward and sits closer to her. 'Hmm, Kirakee, this is not a dream. You are awake,' he whispers in her ear.

Upon hearing this, she freezes, staying very still; her eyes are the only things that can move. Her heart is racing again. She breathes heavily and gulps.

'Don't be afraid. We are not here to cause you any harm,' says Tarkin with an unusually deep voice.

'Yeah, we've been watching you. Stark told us all about you,' Sheena says with a gentle roar.

Stark reassures her. 'It really is okay, Kirakee. They tell you the truth. They are my friends too.'

Her voice quivers, 'Umm, guys, I didn't really mean anything by asking, 'what's on the menu?'

Stark, Tarkin, and Sheena burst out with laughter.

'No, no, we are Fisherterian's,' Sheena says.

'Huh? Fisherterian's?' Tarkin asks.

'Yeah, yeah. We only eat fish,' Sheena giggles.

Tarkin chuckles, 'Yeah, that's mostly true, but I've never heard of it being called 'Fisherterian,' but since you tried to be a plant-eater when we first arrived here, remember how well that went? You ended up being a Vomiterian.'

'Well, I've never heard of a Vomiterian either,' Sheena laughs aloud. 'Anyway, that doesn't make sense. I spewed up the stuff. I didn't eat it!'

Kirakee begins to relax and giggle. 'I believe the term for mainly eating plants is called Vegetarian.'

Stark chuckles, 'How do you know that Kirakee?'

She thinks for a moment, and with a shake of her head, she says, 'I really don't know. I didn't even know that word existed until now either.'

Stark chuckles, 'You guys are so funny. You make me laugh.'

'Oh, my spirit. This is real,' Kirakee whispers.

Stark hears her whisper and responds. 'You can believe it. It's all true.'

Kirakee begins to relax. She is curious and has so many questions to ask. 'How did you all find each other, and why have you become friends?'

'I'll let Tarkin, and Sheena start with that story,' says Stark.

'Okay, take a spot and sit, and get comfortable. We have a story to tell,' says Tarkin.

'We once lived with humans. We were born in a place humans call a Zoo. That's where people came to see animals from all different places around the world. The Zoo had too many animals, and there was no more room for any other newcomers. So, the day we were born, Sheena and me, they were going to destroy us. However, a kind and caring man who was a caretaker at the zoo offered to buy us with money from the zoo owners. The zoo owners sold us to the man who then became our keeper and Master. He saved our lives.

'Our master gave us a home in a large secure cage which also had another area so he could take us outside to play in the sunshine and fresh air.

'Sometimes, our master would take us to his house when we were still young. There were many other houses around where he lived, but when we grew a lot bigger, he had to stop taking us to his home.

'He would come and see us at our pen every day to feed us and walk us around in the outside enclosure, but sometimes when we played with him, we would accidentally hurt him with our claws. Sometimes we were just too rough. He would hide his injuries from other humans in fear that they would take us away from him. He always protected us from trouble. We learned a lot from him and eventually learned to be gentler.

'It cost our master a great deal of money to feed us; therefore, our master found a way for us to earn some money to help buy the food. We became quite famous as we appeared in newspapers, television, and many public appearances for entertainment or advertising. Life was cruising. We were fed well and never had to go hungry.

'However, the authorities came to take us away because there were many humans building houses around our territory, and the people who knew of our existence became concerned about their safety. They were worried that we might escape from our pen and cause harm to them, their children, and their pets. Our master argued with them and asked for some time so he could find another place to make our home. He was only given a short period of time. He eventually came to be very stressed because no one would allow him to rent or buy any other land. They didn't want big animals like us anywhere nearby to where they lived.

'Our master eventually ran out of time to find us a new home, and the authorities were coming to destroy us. So, our master put us in the back of his car and took us away from the danger.

'We travelled for a long time. We watched a few moons come and go, but eventually, tragedy befell us all. Our master lost control of his car on a bend causing the car to roll along the roadside. Sheena and I were thrown from the car, and our master was trapped in the wreckage. We tried to find a way to free him, but eventually, another car began to approach. In fear for our safety, our Master told us to escape into the woods and hide. We did as he said. We watched as our master was taken away in the other car.

'Days and nights passed as we waited for our master to return. Being cold and hungry, we went deeper into the forest in search of food. But as we grew tired and weak, we just didn't know where we were any longer, so we continued in the hope that our Master would return to find us; he never has.'

Tarkin looks sad and hangs down his head.

Stark clears his throat. 'Yes, and when I found Tarkin and Sheena, it was obvious they had been through a very tough time. It was the end of autumn when I found them. As I was passing by a cave, I heard sounds coming from inside. A noise I had never heard before. Out of curiosity, I peeked inside. There I found Tarkin and Sheena lying there. Sheena was moaning and trying to call out to her master. They were skin and bone, starved, and near death. They were weak and dying. I could see they were helpless, and they didn't have any strength left in them.

'Although I didn't know them and wasn't sure of whether they would be of danger to me, I just couldn't just leave them there to die. I sensed they wouldn't cause me any harm. They were in trouble and needed some help. Therefore, I went out hunting and foraging for food to bring back to them. I did this for a few days until they began to gain their strength back once again. When they told me their story, I realized they needed my help. So, when they were strong enough, I took them with me on hunting trips and showed them around the forest, teaching them how to do things.'

'Stark was our Saviour, and he still is,' Tarkin says.

Sheena jumps up and speaks. 'He sure has. We wouldn't even be alive right now if it wasn't for him. He has done so much for us, but I'm afraid to say we suck at a lot of things. The best we can do is catch fish. You know. Fisherterian's! But the best thing of all is that we have all become the very best of friends.'

'Isn't that the truth,' Tarkin says.

Stark smiles and nods. 'I totally agree, and at the near end of every fall, I return here to help them out through the winter months. I've been doing this every winter since I found them.'

'Yeah, thank goodness for that too because we suck at doing anything through that snowy, freezing cold season,' Sheena says with a frown.

Kirakee gets to her feet and straightens up. 'I'll be happy to help you all through the winter. If that's okay with you, Stark?'

'Great! The more help, the better. I really appreciate your offer,' Stark replies.

'Oh, by the way, have you been warned of the increasing dangers down at Two Moon Lake?' Sheena asks.

Kirakee nods, 'Yes, I'm aware of the day and night dangers. Daytime, humans. Night-time, mad wolves,' she sighs.

Sheena looks sad. 'So true. You know, for a very long time, we never seen any humans around the forest until recently. The first time I seen any of them was when I ventured on down to the lake and watched a bear fishing on the lake edge. He made it look easy for catching big fish, so I thought I'd give it a go. So, while I was trying to catch a fish, I was to spot a couple of humans walking alongside the lake edge. I was so surprised. My first thought was, they might be able to show me where our master is.

'I stepped out of the water and then walked towards them. They stopped walking and stared at me for a moment, then turned around and started running, so I then ran after them.

'They were very fast, you know, but I ran as fast as I could so I could follow them, but they stopped and climbed up into a tree,' she frowns. 'I've never seen that before. Our master never did anything like that. I figured that they must be a different kind of breed.

'I waited at the base of the tree for a while until that bear I'd seen down at the lake came running after me like a grumpy old bear with a sore head. Sigh! Never seen those people after that.'

Kirakee and Stark just stare for a moment, then break out into laughter.

'Stranger danger?' Kirakee laughs.

'Yes, I think it was more like they didn't want to be your lunch,' Stark chuckles.

'What do you mean?' says Tarkin

'First, those humans climbed that tree because they were frightened of Sheena. Second, they don't know her and would have thought she was chasing them, intending to hurt them,' says Stark.

Sheena puts her head up and frowns. 'Hurt them? Never deliberately!'

Tarkin silently stares for a moment before he speaks. 'I guess this answers the question of why more humans are coming down to the lake since Sheena was seen. They could possibly be trying to find us. Unfortunately, they're not being friendly about it, though.'

Kirakee gasps. 'We must be more careful now. I've been warned about Two Moon Lake. We all need to stay away from there.'

Stark, Tarkin, and Sheena nod their heads, agreeing with Kirakee.

'It's getting late. Are you going to stay here now, Kirakee?' Stark asks.

She nods. 'Yes. I'll stay for a few sunrises, and then I must return to my family to let them know I'll be staying away for the winter,' she replies.

'Great! Let us show you around. You really must see Tarkin's and Sheena's home. That's where we will be staying through the winter,' Stark says.

Tarkin's and Sheena's den is big and spacious, and on the outside, it is hidden by a lot of shrubs.

Kirakee gasps. 'Wow, this is so much bigger than my family den at Morakee.'

'We have been very fortunate to find this cave,' says Tarkin

'Let us show you where we go every day when there is a clear sky and the sun is at its highest peak,' says Sheena.

They walk down to the riverbank, then climb up on top of one of the largest bolder rocks at the edge of the river.

'Wow, we can see everything from up here. Oh, look, there is my newest home on the other side of the river,' Kirakee says.

'Hmm, yes, we know. We were watching you for some time before you ever got around to making your little den,' Tarkin says

Kirakee gasps. 'You were watching me?'

Tarkin chuckles, 'Sure was. Stark told us all about you.'

She turns and stares at Stark. Feeling a little shy, she tilts her head with a little gush.

She stands up straight and takes a deep breath. 'So why do you make a trip to this rock on sunny days?'

Tarkin looks sad and bows his head down. 'We have been

doing this ever since we lost our master.' He looks back up and takes a deep breath. 'When it's sunny, it's clear, so we can see the forest and river surroundings much better. This is where we wait, look out, and call for him on those days. We miss him very much.'

Sheena moves close to Tarkin and puts her head on his shoulder. 'Yes, we do.'

Kirakee is saddened by their story. 'Aww, so sorry, guys. I guess all we can do now is never give up on hope. He could still find you someday.'

A couple of days pass, and it is time for Kirakee to head back to her family to tell them of her plans. But she decides it would be much safer for her newfound friends if she were to not reveal their identity, fearing the packs may try to drive them out of the Orphaned River.

Trouble Comes

Chapter
7

During her journey home, it doesn't go smoothly. It is becoming late, and a storm is moving in.

She speeds up her pace to avoid the storm, but the storm is picking up speed and power. The winds are so powerful, causing trees and branches to fall, and it blows her backward. The rain is pounding down and hitting her with great force. She is now drenched from the rain, and the environmental conditions are not safe. She shivers and is beginning to feel quite weak.

Just as she is passing a large tree, she sees a hollow in the base, so she moves over to see if it is occupied.

'Thank goodness; no one lives in there. I'll just have to stay in here until the storm passes over,' she thinks.

Inside the hollow of the tree, it is dry. She huddles down and curls up, trying to gather the heat from her body.

While resting in the tree hollow, she has a clear view of the intensity of the storm outside. Suddenly in her view, she sees a light-colored shape swirling around in the wind.

'What is that?' she whispers.

She stands to her feet and sticks her head outside to try and see what is floating around in the wind.

'Hoot, hoot! Hoot, hoot.'

She looks in the direction of the sound, and there, being blown around in all different directions by the wind, is Tick Tock.

'Tick Tock,' she gasps. 'Try and come down here out of the wind and rain,' she calls out.

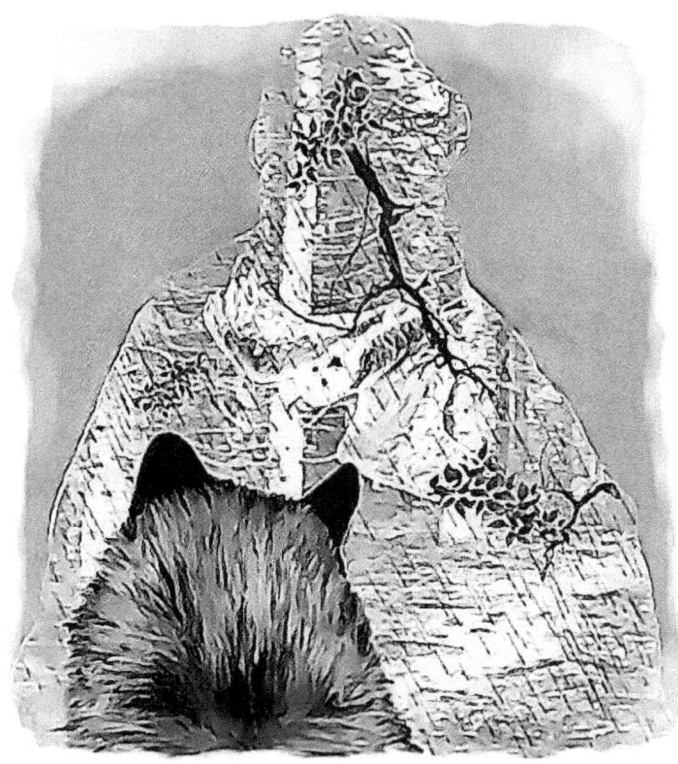

Tick Tock tries a few times, but the wind is so strong; it just keeps blowing him away.

'Hoot, hoot! Hoot, hoot! I'm trying, but I can't.'

'Hang on,' she shouts. 'Oh, sorry, you can't really do that. Umm, I mean, just give me a minute. I'll get something to help you.'

She grabs hold of a broken branch and holds it up as high as she can above her head.

'When you get closer, grab on to this, Tick Tock.'

Tick Tock attempts to grab the branch a couple of times but is blown away again.

'I'm not giving up on you, Tick Tock, so don't you give up on me saving you. Keep trying!'

At last, Tick Tock grabs hold of the branch.

'Now, HANG ON,' Kirakee bellows.

After a bit of a struggle fighting the force of the wind, she finally returns to the hollow with Tick Tock.

'Hoot, hoot! I never thought I'd ever survive that. Thank you, Kirakee, for rescuing me.'

'Wow, Tick Tock! I was worried I'd never see you again. I'm so glad I just happened to be here to bring you to safety.

Kirakee and Tick Tock huddle together for warmth, but because they are drenched by the rain, they shiver uncontrollably until they become so tired and fall asleep.

The sunshine's once again; the storm has passed.

'Hoot, hoot! Wake up, Kirakee.'

Kirakee opens her eyes and jumps to her feet. 'Wow, we've been here all night,' she gasps.

They step outside and see the damage done by the storm. Trees and branches lay all over the ground.

'This is so bad, Tick Tock. I'm so glad we survived that one.' Her thoughts turn to her family. *'I wonder if my family is safe?'*

'I must get going, Tick Tock. I must help my family.'

'Hoot, hoot! I hope they are safe, and I guess you are anxious to get back home to see your brother Conan?'

Kirakee frowns. 'Huh? My brother, Conan. Home?'

Tick Tock looks surprised. 'You don't know?'

'No, I haven't heard anything about my brothers for a very long time.'

'Hoot, hoot. I thought you knew. Your brother came home a few days ago.'

'Oh, my good spirit. I had no idea.' She takes a deep breath and exhales. 'I'll see you later.'

Kirakee runs off; she is so happy to be told of this good news. Conan is alive. She could not be any more excited and happier to get home and see him, but she does worry about why Dasher is not with Conan.

As she approaches her family den, there are fallen trees and branches all over the tracks. Ahead she can see her aunt and father digging around the den entrance.

She calls out. 'Aunty, Father, I'm home.'

They do not look very happy as they look around and stare at her as she approaches.

'Good to see you, Kirakee. As you can see, we have some damage done to our home because of the storm. Could you help us clean this up?' her father asks.

'No problem. I'll get to work as soon as I catch up with Conan. Good news with him being home, but what about Dasher. Where is he?'

'How did you find out about him being home?' asks her aunt.

'A friend told me when I was on my way here.'

Her aunt silently stares at her for a moment. 'Well, you're too late.

He left here yesterday in a hurry so he could avoid the storm.'

Kirakee feels the loss of not seeing him. She has so many questions. 'So where has he gone. Does he know where Dasher is?'

'We will tell you everything soon after we have cleaned up around here,' her aunt says.

Kirakee gets to work and helps clear the damage.

'Okay, that's done. Sit down with us in the sun, and I'll tell you everything you need to know,' her aunt says.
'Okay, as you know, when Dasher became ill and injured, he was captured by a human and then taken away in a cage. Conan followed them to the man's camp. Conan waited nearby, hiding in the woods. He could hear Dasher's howls, and that's when he knew he was alive.

'Conan had to find shelter, and while he was looking around, he met a she-wolf with her pup. He took care of them while he stayed nearby to the camp area where your Dasher was being held.

'After many moons, the human spotted Conan outside the camp, but instead of harming him, he threw food to Conan and his new companion and her pup. That human showed he didn't mean them any harm, so Conan and his companions felt safe to stay where they were and hopefully see Dasher again.

'Many more moons passed, and to their relief, the man brought the cage out with Dasher inside. He opened it and let Dasher go free so he could join Conan and his new family.'

'But why aren't they here now?' Kirakee asks

'Well, although the man has healed Dasher, he still isn't very well. He only stayed with Conan shortly after but without any explanation, he went in another direction, and the last thing they had seen of him was he had gone over to the south side of the Orphaned River, but Conan was heading there when he left here.'

Kirakee's eyes pop open wide. 'Oh, really! Umm, maybe I might

71

see them. I have something to tell both of you.'

'I hope it's good news?' says her father.

'Yes! It's good news, but I think you won't like it.'

Her aunt fidgets around a bit; she looks a bit uncomfortable. 'Okay, I just don't want to hear any more bad news.'

Kirakee straightens up. 'No, it's not bad for me. I'm moving down to the Orphaned River and will be living with a few friends for the winter.'

Her aunt looks shocked. 'But why on earth would you choose to live down there of all places?' she growls. 'Okay, okay, you do what you want. You are old enough to take care of yourself, but remember, I have warned you about Orphaned River.'

'It's not a problem, Aunty. I have been there and now know the area very well, and my friends are big and strong. I know I'll be safe with them,' Kirakee says.

'Okay, it's your choice, and if that's really what you feel you have to do, then there is nothing more we can say,' says her father.

Kirakee puts her head on her father's shoulder. 'Thank you. I will return from time to time to see the family. I'm not going to be that far away.'

Her aunt stands up and walks away.

Her father sits up straight. 'I'll let you know as much as I know before you go. I don't think your brother will ever be returning here again. Well, not unless he gets his health right. I heard your aunt and Dasher had an argument before he went missing. He then began following her around, asking her the same things repeatedly. Apparently, this created more tension.'

'What was he saying?' Kirakee asks.

'He was following your aunt around asking her, Do you even care about any of us, aunt? Have you ever cared about anyone else other than yourself and Morana? Your aunt never answered his questions. She just walked away.'

'That is so awful. Poor Dasher,' Kirakee says sadly.

Kirakee is worried. She hangs her head feeling sad.

'I hope he will be alright?'

'Don't worry, Kirakee. He is in good care. Your brother Conan will find him and take good care of him.'

Kirakee nods. 'I believe that too.'

A couple of days later, her father and aunt farewell her on her new journey.

As she is walking away from them, she stops and turns around. 'When you see Conan and Dasher again, please let them know I'm thinking of them and miss them very much. I hope to see them again, someday soon.'

Her father nods in agreement, while her aunt just ignores again by walking away.

The Rise of Man

Chapter
8

On her return journey to the river, she meets up with her forest friends and tells them what she is doing. They are happy for her and jump up and down with excitement.

She is excited about her new adventure but is also concerned about the winter season setting in. The realization of the job she has ahead of her will be challenging. Taking care of Tarkin and Sheena is going to be a whole new experience, but she knows she will learn so much more from Stark, which will help her too. Knowing this brings her a sense of comfort.

The winter sets in, and it makes everything feel tough. The snowfall is heavier than any other winter she has known.

Stark and Kirakee work extremely hard to take care of Tarkin, Sheena, as well as themselves. They are scavenging for anything they can find to help them survive.

The days pass by quickly until late winter arrives. Kirakee has been worrying about her family, so she makes a trip home to Morakee to see if everyone is doing okay.

Back in Morakee, she is greeted with more news about some changes with bad news. Kirakee's sister, Morana, has moved out of the family den into another den with a he-wolf. The bad news that disturbs Kirakee greatly is that her brother Dasher had taken off again after Conan had found him on the south side of the Orphaned River. They had an argument, but the argument was between Conan's new mate and Dasher.

Dasher had ceased to eat well. His poor diet caused him to become aggressive.

Conan had reported that Dasher had been spotted somewhere in the territory but said, 'Dasher has lost the plot.'

This news stresses Kirakee.

Dasher is still in the territory on the other side of the Orphaned River. She does not want to see him while he is in bad shape, fearing he could stir up trouble with her new friends, Tarkin, Sheena, and Stark.

She loves her brother and cares for his safety, but she fears for both parties' well-being.

The only thought on her mind right now is to return to the Orphaned River to explain to her friends that her brother Dasher is in a troubled way, so if they see him, they should let her know, and she will take care of him.

It is time for Kirakee to leave Morakee and head back to the river. Her aunt and father inform her of an upcoming wolf gathering event that they are putting on for her sister Morana. They ask if she will be able to come back to join the gathering.

A few weeks later, the snow has completely melted, and Springtime has begun again. It is time for the wolf gathering in honor of her sister, so she heads back to Morakee. Upon her arrival, Morana is busy socializing with everyone else. Kirakee does not get the chance to talk to her sister.

A couple of days later, she decides to take a trip to Morana's den after arranging a visit a few days earlier. She has not seen where she is living yet, but it would be a suitable time to catch up and spend some time with her before she returns to the river.

'This is a good place, Morana. I like it.'

Morana is busy arranging mealtime. 'It's alright, I guess. I can't talk now. I need to get this done.'

Just as Kirakee senses her sister does not have time for her, a couple of other wolves turn up. Morana is more thrilled to see them than she has been to see Kirakee.

'We're going to have a meal now. You may as well go. I don't have enough to share it with you as well,' Morana says to Kirakee.

Kirakee feels she is not welcome, and her sister prefers to share a meal with other wolves instead of her own sister.

Feeling disappointed her sister would treat her that way after the effort she has made to return for her event, she decides it would be best to return to her friends back at the Orphaned River.

All the way back to the river, she is disturbed about her home visit. As she walks, she does not take notice of the surroundings because she walks with her head hanging down.

Thoughts are running through her head. *I came all the way back for her event and made the journey to see her and her new home, and she doesn't even care. She didn't care that I was there. She didn't even show she wanted me to be around. Just plain rude!'*

Just as she approaches closer to the river, the sun is at its peak, and she knows Sheena and Tarkin will be down at the river very soon to look out and call out for their Master as they have done every other day when the sky is clear.

Her spirit begins to pick up. She has missed her friends and looks forward to seeing them again. As she begins to approach the river to cross, she hears some noise. She stops and investigates and looks around to find where the sound is coming from.

'Gasp!'

She becomes terrified. Close to where she stands are a few humans, sitting down alongside the riverbank.

'Oh, no, I have to warn Tarkin, Stark, and Sheena before they come down to the river,' she whispers.

For a moment, she looks around to see if she can find another crossing on the river so she can get to the other side without the men seeing her, but the only spot is much further upstream.

Just as she begins to head upriver, she sees something in the side of her vision.

'Gasp! Oh, no, it's Sheena and Tarkin. I'm too late; they are going to be seen,' she whispers.

Wondering what she can do to let them know of the danger before they call out for their Master and attract the attention of the men, she suddenly comes up with the only idea she can think of doing.

She begins running toward the humans and growling so she can distract them from seeing her friends. The men jump up and begin shouting at her as she gets closer to them. As she runs past them, there are loud bangs.

Bullets fly, only just missing her.

She turns around and runs in another direction, but the humans come running after her, shooting at her.

Her plan to distract the humans is working, but now her own life is in jeopardy.

They are relentless in their pursuit. She blindly runs into the thickness of the shrubs and forest, not knowing what is ahead of her, and then, thud! She falls into a deep hole in the ground.

The men are still looking for her; she can hear their voices.

As she lays at the bottom of the deep hole, she feels like she has spared her life from the bullets, but she knows she is not going to be able to get out of the hole as it's far too deep.

As she sits at the bottom of what now feels like her grave, she hears growling and screaming. Then silence falls upon the woods. The humans have gone.

She tries to climb out of the hole, jumping up and down, trying to reach the top of the edge but continuously falls back down.

Day and night pass, she is contemplating her destiny, convinced she will never be free of where she is if no one else ever finds her.

She is growing hungry, thirsty, and tired.

She curls up, shivering from the cold night and howls during the day in the hope that someone will hear and rescue her.

The humans have moved on quickly. Tarkin, Sheena, and Stark have begun searching for Kirakee. They have been looking for her for most of the day and are beginning to give up on the hope of ever finding her alive. But they are determined to find her body, whether dead or alive.

Not too far into the distance, they hear a faint howl.

'Can you hear that?' says Stark.

They stand still for a moment, making their own kind of silence.

'Listen!'

'Yes, yes, I can hear that,' Tarkin says.

They start running towards the howls. As they run in the direction of the noise, a sudden silence falls, and nowhere can they see Kirakee.

'I'm so sure this is where the call was coming from,' Stark says while spinning around.

Stark feels sure that she is not far away, as he can smell her scent, so he must call out for her.

He howls, 'Kirakee.'

Kirakee can clearly hear Stark. 'I'm down here,' she calls out with a weak voice.

Stark, Sheena, and Tarkin quickly move over to the hole in the ground.

'Thank goodness you're still alive,' Tarkin says.

'You'll have to find a way to get me out of here. I've tried, but the hole is too deep.'

Stark begins to dig frantically at one side of the edge of the hole.

Dirt is flying everywhere, but he notices he is the only one digging, so he stops, sits down, and looks at Tarkin and Sheena. 'So, why are you just sitting there? Why aren't you helping?'

'Well, we are not wolves, and our own kind don't dig up the earth,' Sheena smugly says.

'Oh, is that right! So, are you just going to sit there watching me while you groom yourselves?' Stark asks

Tarkin chuckles, 'Yeah, yeah, that's something Sheena would do!'

'Well?' frowns Stark.

'Okay, okay, but this isn't something we've ever had any practice at doing, so just be prepared for you to wear a lot more dirt on you, too,' Sheena says.

They all begin digging until they have dug deep enough to create a ledge that Kirakee will be able to jump up on, giving her a chance to be closer to the top of the hole.

She tries to jump up, but she is not strong enough and continues to slip back down.

'This is not going to work. I just don't have the strength to do it,' she cries out. 'Is there another way,' she asks.

'I have an idea! Give me a moment,' replies Tarkin.

Tarkin speaks to the others and informs them he will jump down into the hole and try and help Kirakee out.

'Move back; I'm coming down,' he shouts out to Kirakee.

Tarkin jumps down into the hole with Kirakee, gently grabs her around the neck, then jumps up onto the ledge. Sheena then leans down into the hole, grabs Kirakee off the ledge, and brings her out.

'Woo! Woo! We did it. We did it. We got you out,' Sheena says while they all jump around with excitement.

Kirakee pants; she is exhausted but overwhelmed with gratitude. 'You are the best of friends in the whole world. I can't believe it; you did it!'

'I know. I'm proud of ourselves and so happy you are safe now after all you did to protect us,' Stark smiles. 'However, there is someone else we need to thank too.'

'Oh! Who?' Kirakee frowns.

'Your brother, Dasher, and the mean old brown bear,' Stark smiles.

'What? My brother and bear. How is that possible?' Kirakee cannot contain her emotions. The news overwhelms her. She whimpers.

'I'll answer that,' Sheena steps forward. 'I saw all that had happened before today, so I can tell you everything.'

'Go on, Sheena. Please tell me.' Kirakee shakes her head.

Sheena proceeds. 'Your brother has been venturing onto both sides of the Orphaned River over the past week, and at one point, the human hunters were about to shoot the brown bear, but your brother intervened and distracted the hunters until the bear was able to escape.'

Kirakee gasps. She is in shock to hear this news. She gathers her thoughts. 'But was Dasher injured by the hunters?'

'No, not at all,' Sheena smiles. 'However, Dasher has been closely watching the hunters since they arrived. He was there when they began shooting at you, so he came out of hiding, and once again, he distracted the hunters to save you. Attracting the hunters' attention was to make them come after him, and they did.

But while they were in pursuit of your brother, the brown bear saw the trouble Dasher was in, so he intervened too.

That big old grumpy bear saved your brother's life by chasing away the hunters.'

Kirakee hangs her head and whimpers. Mixed emotions of sadness, happiness, and pride consume her. Grateful for all who have cared for her, and knowing her brother and friends are safe means everything to her right now.

For many weeks after, they often talk about those days.

They have become more cautious with their visit to the river since men have been there, so they begin exploring different parts of the woods.

While exploring, they find an open valley outside the forest edge and spend days roaming, running, and laughing together.

The threat of man did not come back to the river, but they had learned their lesson to know to hide from them. They sense the river is not going to be the best for safety due to the lack of freedom to fish out in the open is going to take a toll on Tarkin and Sheena. Stark decides to offer a safer place to live, deeper in the woods.

They all travel for days while dodging any potential threats until they find an area that has a smaller river than that of the Orphaned. At least they will be able to do their fishing here. Not far away, they find another small unoccupied cave for shelter.

Stark and Kirakee leave for the sake of completing Stark's mission and promise to return to their big cat friends by the return of the following winter.

Kirakee and Stark travel into many parts of the woods she has never known about. They visit many wolf packs so Stark can share his story.

Kirakee has grown and become much stronger. She has nearly reached the full size that is normal for a she-wolf of her age, but she still is a little smaller than the rest.

Her eyes sparkle, and her inconsistent drooping ears have begun to stand up more often.

Her confidence has grown.

Being friends with Stark, Tarkin, and Sheena has shown her a love she has never known before.

She now feels brave enough to believe she can make positive choices to start living her own life now as a mature she-wolf.

New Beginnings

Chapter
9

She has mixed feelings about leaving her friends, Stark, Tarkin, and Sheena, but she is excited to share her stories of adventure with her sister Morana. For once, she has something interesting to talk about that just does not involve everything about Morana.

Morana has moved back into Morakee after things have not worked out with her new mate because he likes to shift around with other wolves.

Not being happy that she has had to leave her new home territory because of all the new friends she has made through her now ex-mate, she is feeling quite glum.

Kirakee sees this as an opportunity to brighten things up by telling her some bright, exciting stories.

She takes Morana to a quiet spot and gets her to sit down. She begins telling her sister of her new adventures.

'I don't care,' Morana snaps.

'What? Why would you say that?' Kirakee snaps back.

Morana lunges forward. 'I don't like you!'

'What do you mean?' Kirakee snaps.

Morana lunges forward, striking Kirakee angrily. 'I hate you. I don't like the way you are now. I preferred you the way you were before.'

Kirakee snaps and strikes back. They begin to fight.

Their father is nearby, so he runs over and breaks them up. 'Hey, hey, you two, cut it out. There is no need for that.'

Kirakee and Morana scatter and do not talk to each other after their encounter.

Kirakee is confused and worried about how her sister thinks of her.

This does not make her feel comfortable being around her at all evermore.

With having to acknowledge there is a problem with her sister because the tension continues between them, she feels it would be best to avoid her and find a new place she could live in of her own.

While seeking a new home, she receives word that another she-wolf is also seeking to move out of her family den. She creates an alliance with the other wolf, and they begin to share a new den together.

Things are good. It is peaceful, and she feels free to be herself. She also likes her new friend and gets on quite well with her.

However, her aunt and her sister Morana are not pleased Kirakee has grown stronger over the past few seasons since it goes against their plan to make sure she endures many hardships so it will make her weaker and cause her to have no confidence to become a leader.

A few days later, her aunt comes to visit, but her visit is not just about seeing her new home but rather about a request for Kirakee to have her sister Morana move in with them.

Kirakee's first thoughts are of concern and doubt. *'This is not good. She doesn't like me. She might cause trouble. I would rather not have to live with her.'*

Kirakee attempts to divert her aunt's request by telling her that they had not planned to share their new home with anyone else.

Her aunt becomes annoyed and angry. 'Well, your sister wants to move in with you.
Also, your father and I are getting old, and we would like to have our own home to ourselves for a change.
It would be good for both of you to live in your own place together. Then, you can take care of each other.'

Kirakee is not feeling comfortable to be having an argument with her aunt, so she cannot disagree while she does all the talking.

A few days pass, and Morana moves into Kirakee's new home.

Already, Morana has her own ideas for what part of the den she wants, so she is given her own space while Kirakee and her den mate share a bigger space together.

Tension is in the air. She knows this is not a healthy situation, but she tries to convince herself that it's the right thing to do.

Tension continues between her and her sister.

Kirakee feels she must be cautious around Morana but hopes she will accept her in good time.

Good news arrives. Their sister Cloud has given birth

to another pup, a little he-wolf this time.

The bad news is that the father of her pup had become a thief, stealing from the rest of Cloud's pack, and he has been banished from Cloud's home territory.

This news causes everyone to have mixed feelings.

Kirakee hangs her head down and shakes it. *'Poor Cloud. It's another disappointment for her. Another partner letting her down. It must be so hard on her.'*

Every time they know Cloud visits, they make sure they are there to see her and her new pup. Kirakee looks forward to talking to Cloud. Cloud really understands her, and she completely understands Kirakee's hardships with her sister Morana.

Cloud has her own opinion of how she views Kirakee's and Morana's relationship.

'She is jealous of you,' Cloud says to Kirakee.

Kirakee is surprised. 'Jealous of me. But why? I don't see why she would be.'

'Well, she has always been an attention seeker, and she doesn't like it when you get attention,' Cloud replies.

This news confuses Kirakee. She has never known this kind of thing. Not even she has acted in such a way toward any of her family members, but it does make her question a lot of things about what her sister has done and said to her.

She wonders if jealousy could be what motivates Morana.

Kirakee is again feeling like everything is the same as when she lived at home with her parents.

Morana and Kirakee have some good days amongst many days of fighting. The fights and arguments break out when Morana is not entirely getting her own way.
She gets aggressive when she is not placed in the position of

dominance. Therefore, Kirakee needs to be more submissive to her.

On some days, Kirakee just gets so fed up with it and does what she feels is best for herself by being confident enough to stand up for her own position in their den. This does not help matters much because her sister would rather Kirakee be like the mouse she was before she had lived at the Orphaned River.

The fights and arguments have Kirakee feeling like she is walking around on eggshells most of the time, and it is beginning to take a toll on her. It is making her feel down in the dumps. At this stage, she is feeling the pressure of being trapped in a really bad situation.

A few weeks later, Morana is arguing with her first ex-partner about her wanting to see her old friends she had made while she was with him back in his wolf pack clan.

He refuses to let her return. She is very upset. Kirakee figures she could be of some help if she talks to him as she is not emotionally involved with him.

'Morana, please let me talk to him. I might be able to persuade him to think differently, so he will let you return to visit.'

Kirakee is confident she can make a difference and help her sister out with this problem that is bothering her.

She talks to Morana's ex-mate, and he is very polite and listens to what she has to say, and eventually agrees to let Morana visit the clan.

Kirakee is pleased; she has been able to help her sister out and is happy to tell her the news.

Morana fires up at the news instead of being thankful and happy. 'You like him, don't you? You've probably had something going on with him all this time.'

'No, no, that is not true at all, Morana,' Kirakee pleads.

Morana does not want to believe anything Kirakee says, so she just continues accusing Kirakee of betrayal and dishonesty. She loses the plot and goes on and on for days, throwing anything up at Kirakee that she does not like about her.

A couple of days later, Kirakee has had enough, so she starts to strike back. They aggressively fight.

Kirakee feels she is losing herself—losing her newfound confidence and self-esteem—and becomes very depressed. She becomes so depressed that she wants to give up on everything.

The only thing she can think to do is talk to their parents about what is happening and ask them to help solve the problem. So, she goes to their den and asks for help.

Upon them hearing what she tells them, her aunt becomes angry and snaps. 'Don't come to us every time you've got a problem telling us all about it. Both of you are old enough to work it out for yourselves without involving us. Now leave us alone,' her aunt says angrily.

Her aunt turns her back on her as if she is just being a nuisance instead of taking notice of what the problem is doing to her.

Kirakee looks at her father in bewilderment and wonders why he is not saying anything. She questions, 'Father?'

'I'm sorry, Kirakee, maybe your aunt has a point. It's only your sister, and most likely, she will come to her senses soon. There is no reason for her to be like that. I'm sure she will improve for the better.'

Kirakee's father looks sincere. She respects his words and desperately wants to believe he is right.

The following day, Morana finds out Kirakee had gone to their parent's den to seek help and was refused. This just adds more fuel for Morana to criticize and run Kirakee down. Day after day, Morana insults, assaults, and taunts her.

Morana now has the idea that she can get away with anything in her head. Not even her parents would bother to reproof her.

Kirakee is convinced she cannot take any more. She lays down and wants to exit out of the world.

She is whimpering and wishing she would disappear.

For a few days, she stays immobilized in the same spot while Morana walks around the den calling her names.

Morana knows what Kirakee is doing and has no reason to be concerned. Her part of the plan is working. She comes over to Kirakee while lying down, crying, and begins assaulting her while she lies on the den floor.

Morana snaps and continues to insult. 'Go you stupid she-wolf, Witches poo. I don't care if you disappear. I wish you would.'

'Go away, death breath,' Kirakee shouts.

Morana leaves the den and does not return until a few days later, and upon her return, she continues to be aggressive.

She looks at Kirakee and notices she is still surviving.

'Oh, no, Witches poo, it's a shame you're still here. Just thought I'd come back and have a look to see if you've disappeared yet,' she smugly says.

Morana leaves, and Kirakee is stunned that her own sister could be so cruel. This disgusts her and makes her angry.

Kirakee realizes the reality of it all. *'She really does hate me. What a horrible, wicked creature she is. She would rather I don't exist. Well, she really is not worth it. Not worth my life.'*

Feeling weak and worn out, she struggles to get to her feet. She must now do all she can to save her own life. She has not eaten or drunk anything in a few days, so she needs to build her strength.

The first thing she does is go down to the nearby stream and drink water, then scavenge for food.

She begins to build her strength once again, but she dreads her sister returning and what will come next with her. She feels sickened and extremely anxious.

When her sister returns, they do not speak to each other. Kirakee tries to keep out of her sister's way. This tends to keep the peace for now, but she can see a certain kind of defeat in Morana's face, almost as if she has lost something.

Times are tough, and sometimes scavenging for food is a big task. This puts a lot more strain on the members of her den. Arguments break out until their den mate has had enough of it all.

'I'm so sick of all the arguments and the fighting. I've got to get away from it all,' she snaps.

Eventually, she moves out of the den and finds herself another place to live.

Kirakee decides to go out often to avoid her sister.

Morana just is not making her feel comfortable being at home because she looks angry all the time.

On one of her outings attending a wolf gathering, Kirakee meets a young wolf named 'Mist.'

Instantly, they are drawn to each other. However, Mist comes from a wolf pack way out of their territory, and although they whip up a bond together, issues arise because of him mingling with a foreign wolf pack.

Kirakee falls for Mist. She looks at him with admiration. His eyes are amazing, and they change colour with his moods. Romance is in the air.

The more time she spends with Mist, the more she is to learn about him and his pack.

His pack are extremely strict, and because he still is a young wolf, he does not hold a position in the pack. Therefore, the lack of standing does not give him the power to say if he can join another territory of wolves. That means for Mist to have a mate in his life, he needs to have someone of his own pack, or if not, he would have to work harder to gain acceptance from his own. This issue is posing a problem for Kirakee and Mist to be together.

Kirakee does not see him a lot as he spends time away living in his own territory, and she doubts whether they will ever be able to be together properly. She talks about this to her friends, expressing her fears.

A few months pass by, and she is beginning to feel different in herself. Something is changing, but she is not quite sure why she feels so tired and hungry quite often.

Not understanding what is happening to her, she visits the Legend wolf pack to seek a solution.

'Ha, Kirakee, you're pregnant…You're going to be a mother!' The Legend member smiles.

Her eyes pop wide open. 'Are you sure?'

'Oh, yes! I'd expect you'll have this done very soon,' he says

Kirakee is shocked. Questions race through her mind. *Can I really expect Mist to be committed since he won't leave his own pack? I know he can only support me and the new arrival if I am accepted by his pack? Will he want me to try and be accepted? Do I really want to join his pack? Will he really want us to join?'*

Before she tells Mist, she tells her friends.

It looks like Morana is not anywhere in sight, but she is nearby eavesdropping. She is unimpressed about the news, and it angers her.

Soon after, Kirakee tells her father and aunt, and her aunt is especially not happy. Her father is concerned about the difference in territories.

'We think it would be a bad idea for you to join Mist's pack. We think you should forget about the whole idea,' her father says.

Even though her aunt is not happy, she expresses a different opinion because she sees it as a good way to remove Kirakee from the territory.

'This would be an especially good thing for Kirakee. A change of duties might be all she needs.'

Kirakee's father looks at Kirakee's aunt with confusion. 'What are you talking about? That does not fit with anything about our territory rules. Her leaving is another pack member less here and will not contribute to the strength of our packs.'

Kirakee is beginning to see her situation as the beginning of arguments, and it is the last thing she needs to happen. 'Please, don't argue. I will sort things out and do the right thing.'

As soon as she comes up with a solution, she musters up the courage to send a messenger wolf to find Mist and let him know she is looking for him because she has something she needs to talk to him about.

She is totally confused about what to do; she thinks about how she will break the news to Mist.

Because of her thoughts of uncertainty and her father's disapproval, she is finding it difficult to make the right decision.

She really needs to hear what Mist thinks and find out what Mist wants. This will help her know what the best thing is to do, and in her heart, she knows she could not be any happier if Mist were to say he wants them to be a part of his life.

Mist arrives and stands like a soldier at attention before Kirakee while she sits looking up at him.

Kirakee nervously takes a deep breath. 'I have something I need to tell you, and I'm not sure of what to do. Maybe this won't be an easy situation? But... I'm pregnant!'

Mist stares in silence for several seconds, trying to process the news. He takes a deep breath and then speaks. 'What do you want to do about it?' he asks.

'I'm not sure what I'm meant to do about it, Mist. You tell me, and then I will know?'

Mist does not spare a moment to reply. 'I'll have to do what's required by my pack. I'll do what I can to support, and...'

Before he finishes his sentence, Morana calls out from her part of the den. She has been listening to Kirakee and Mist.

'Mist, Mist, come here.'

Mist walks towards Morana, leaving Kirakee sitting in anticipation. She is anxious to hear the rest of what Mist was going to say.

Several minutes later, Mist emerges from Morana's part of the den. And without saying another word to Kirakee, he walks straight for the den entrance.

Kirakee is stunned and wonders why he is leaving.

'So, what are you doing?' she asks.

He slows his pace and looks over his shoulder. 'Don't worry about it. Just forget the whole thing.'

Mist then picks up his pace and quickly leaves the den.

Kirakee is lost for words and sits stunned and hurt. Questions run through her mind; *'What did he mean by that? Why did he leave without finishing what he was going to say? Why did Morana want to speak to him, and what did she say?'*

She is suspicious of her sister since she does not trust her, but because of the tension between them, she does not feel it's safe enough to ask her about what she said to Mist. Something was not right, and Kirakee sensed it, but she plans to find out what was said when she sees Mist next time.

A few weeks pass by, and she does not see or hear anything from Mist, but she knows he is safe and well because she has heard reports of him being sighted around. She is bothered that he has not come to speak to her again. Her heart is breaking.

As the days pass, it is increasingly difficult for Kirakee to deal with an obvious problem with her sister. She spends a lot more time resting in her den, making sure she avoids Morana.

One day, just as she is walking into her rest area, Morana confronts her and begins an argument. This is strange to Kirakee, as she cannot figure out what has happened to cause her sister to be so cranky since she has been keeping out of her way.

What Kirakee does not know is that Morana got scolded by her own mother for sending Mist away because it was against her mother's plan to rid Kirakee from Morakee. Morana had not seen her mother beforehand to hear the plan. She had just acted upon her own feelings of jealousy.

'What is wrong with you?' Kirakee asks

Her sister continues to snap. But then she does the most unthinkable thing—she pushes Kirakee up against a rock, causing a mighty crash to her stomach.

Kirakee is outraged that she would do such a thing to her while she is pregnant.

'Why did you do that?' she snaps. 'I'm pregnant, you wicked thing. Get out! Get out!' she shouts.

Morana does not say another word. She walks away in silence, leaves the den, and never returns.

A couple of days later, an old friend of her sister who previously had a fall out with Morana stays with Kirakee. Her friend has a loving mother, and she helps with food and eventually gives Kirakee a place to live.

During the time at their new home, they have problems with some wolves running around outside the den, creating noises in the dark and causing rocks to fall around the entrance. This makes them nervous and feel unsafe. It is obvious that someone does not want them to be there, so Kirakee and her friend leave the den and return to the centre of Morakee.

Upon her return to Morakee, Kirakee must deal with her aunt because she complains about the prospects of having a new pup in the family. And since her aunt does not want to have to deal with it, she encourages Kirakee to seek out a new place of her own further away.

News comes from Morana that she is now pregnant and expecting a pup a short time after Kirakee is to give birth to her own.

When her sister Morana had left Kirakee after their fight, she had gone off and found a new mate.

Now that Morana is pregnant, it influences a common ground between the sisters to communicate.

Reluctantly, Kirakee allows bygones to be bygones. It is now all about survival and having a safe place to give birth and bring up her new addition to her own family.

A Mother's Love

Chapter 10

Eventually, she finds a suitable spot to create her own den and digs out the earth under a fallen tree. It is just big enough for her and her expected offspring. It seems safe.

The time has drawn close for giving birth, and she seeks out Mist to let him know. She hopes he will be involved in some way.

Finally, she speaks to Mist. She can hardly speak, her breath is short, and nerves are making her voice quiver.

'Hello, Mist, I've been wanting to talk to you to let you know that I'm due to give birth very soon.'

Mist pauses for a moment before he speaks. 'Ha, is that right? I thought this wouldn't be happening yet.'

'No, it's not that long away now. I thought you'd like to know, so you can come to see our new pups.'

Mist doesn't say anything else and just walks away.

Kirakee's heart sinks, and all she can think *is, 'he doesn't care.'*

Within a few days of seeing Mist, she goes into labour and gives birth to a beautiful male pup. She names him 'Alfa Noon.' His name represents many things of importance: His name also means, 'Alpha,' for representing leader and first, since he is her first born and a beginning to her new life.

He is also born at the highest peak of the sun, at noon. She strongly senses he will be a leader. He is the light of her life.

He is the only pup she births—unlike her mother, who birthed three pups, but two of the pups became ill and died straight after birth, leaving Kirakee as the only surviving pup. This pattern of only birthing one surviving pup is commonplace around the wolf pack territories of late.

Mist receives word of the arrival of his new son and comes to see him. As he sits before his newborn, he looks over Alfa Noon, checking him all over. Mist chooses not to speak. He just quietly stares at Alfa Noon's tiny face. He is uncomfortable and looks awkward, not knowing what to say.

Kirakee's father is there as well, so he attempts to make conversation with Mist to help ease his discomfort. Kirakee just hopes he will be able to find some joy or pride in his newborn son like she does.

She is finding it difficult to speak to him because she is so nervous. Her thoughts are filled with concern and empathy. *'How hard this must be for him because I'm not of his own pack, and his own don't even know about us. How I wish I could share my feelings of pride with him and make him smile.'*

One week passes, and she does not hear a word about Mist. She is now nurturing their pup alone and is concluding that she should not expect any support.

She even begins to not speak about who Alfa Noon's father is because she feels she should protect Alfa Noon from other territory clan members; she fears they will make him a target of criticism because his father is from another territory.

Even though it makes her heart ache at the thought of not having Mist in their life, it is a situation she does not make lightly, but rather with a heavy heart. She still does not give up on the hope of things changing for the better one day, though. Maybe someday soon, he will be able to become a part of their life.

With that hope, she believes he will eventually try to see Alfa

Noon often, and with that, she will be able to ask him those nagging questions that are constantly in her thoughts. *'Why did he walk out on me? What did my sister Morana say? Why has he gone so cold towards me?'*

It is time for them to move to a bigger den now that Alfa Noon has grown stronger.

Times get tough, and she is becoming weak from not eating regularly. The place they live in is ant-infested, and she is constantly concerned about the ants crawling over Alfa Noon.

Her little pup is only a few weeks old and has become extremely ill. Kirakee has become so weak and sick, too, that she must crawl across the ground to attend to her pup.

'Why isn't my little one getting any better?' she would wonder with worry.

A few days pass, and they both are still terribly ill, so she struggles out of the den with Alfa Noon to seek out the 'Legend' wise wolves in the hope they will be able to help.

When they arrive at the Legends territory, several of the members gather around to check out her son.

One wise wolf says, 'Alfa Noon might not get well. He is too weak, and he might fade away.'

As Kirakee looks at her beautiful son, she wonders what she has done wrong. *'Is there anything I could have done to save my son from this terrible problem? How could this be happening to him.'*

She does not want to believe the wise wolf is right about Alfa Noon fading away, so she stays in their territory for a few days. They provide her with a few small meals, and although she is gaining back some strength, the amount of food is not enough to help her produce enough milk to feed Alfa Noon. So, she must do her own work—scavenging for food. She is determined to do all she can to save her beautiful son.

On her arrival back from food scavenging, one of the 'Legend' members reports of a young he-wolf entering their territory and asking about Alfa Noon. He said the stranger only stayed briefly to see him.

Kirakee knows this must have been Mist. Her heart leaps at the thought of Mist seeing their pup again. Her hopes of Mist acknowledging their son without pressure is all she can hope for now.

For the next ten days, she does all that she can to help her son get well. Slowly and gradually, he is starting to become stronger every day. On day ten, he miraculously recovers from the illness that had threatened his life.

The Legends members put his recovery down to Kirakee's healthy milk supply.

Kirakee is so happy and relieved to have her little son fit and well again.

Now that he is so much stronger to travel, Kirakee
Leaves the Legend territory with Alfa Noon and returns to their own home.

As she intently stares at Alfa Noon, her thoughts wander back to a time when she could not even look after herself, let alone imagine counting one pup as being a part of her life. Alfa Noon has changed that for her, and even though she has decided not to admit it to anyone, she loves Alfa Noon's father, Mist, unconditionally as much as she loves Alfa Noon. Their son is a part of that love, and no matter what, he is now the reason for her living.

Once again, after she returns to her den, Morana begins to invade Kirakee's space, and although it appears her sister is doing it with good intentions, Kirakee just cannot trust her.

Kirakee learns that Morana has seen Mist around. He has been friends with a few of her sister's territory clan members. Morana offers to encourage Mist to come and visit Alfa Noon. Kirakee cannot refuse such a sentiment and agrees for Morana to take on the task even though she does not feel comfortable with doing this because it just gives Morana more control over her situation.

Once again, what Kirakee does not know is that Morana plans to reunite Mist and Kirakee so she can carry through with her mother's original plan for Kirakee to move out of Morakee and live with Mist far away.

A few days later, Kirakee hears a noise outside her den, and she goes out to investigate. To her surprise, it is Mist.

'I was told you want me to come around to see Alfa Noon.'

Kirakee is nervous and a little lost for words. 'Umm, yes. He is awake right now. Come on in.'

Mist sits with Alfa Noon, checking him out but does not say anything.

Kirakee does her best to make conversation. 'He looks more and more like you every day.'

Mist turns and looks at his son again and smiles.

Kirakee informs him about the time their son was sick and the little things he does now. In her head, she is thinking about the things she wants to ask Mist, but she does not want to pounce on him so soon with questions. She plans to wait for a little longer and then ask him before he leaves.

Just as she is making her plan to wait a little longer into his visit to ask him the questions, he announces, 'I've got be leaving now.'

'Oh, okay! Already?' Kirakee asks.

Mist insists he has things to do, leaving Kirakee feeling strained as she does not get the chance to ask him questions.

A few weeks later, her sister Morana is now due for the birth of her own pup, and due to the father of her pup disappearing, their parents help make a den close by to where Kirakee lives. Kirakee is not comfortable with having Morana living next to her, as she still feels some tension between them.

Morana gives birth to only one pup, and since the birth of her new pup, she has been very placid, and for the first time since the birth, the sisters are communicating more like sisters.

Kirakee and Morana visit each other's dens each day, and they share the same interest in being mothers.

A few weeks pass, and Kirakee discovers that not all things have changed for the better when she confronts Morana about the food supplies, she has taken from her without asking.

Kirakee feels angered by what she sees. 'What are you doing? That belongs to me! You're stealing from me again.'

Morana snaps back. 'No, I haven't. It's mine.'

'No, it's not. I can see that it's mine,' Kirakee growls. 'I'm sick of you always helping yourself to my things. You haven't changed,' she snaps.

Morana returns aggression. She is standing on a hilltop with her own pup, and without another word, she knocks down a bunch of dangerously large rocks, so they will deliberately hit Kirakee and Alfa Noon. The rocks just miss landing on them.

Kirakee is shocked, angered, and horrified. 'You just caused those rocks to come down so they would harm us. How could you? You're a mad wolf. Don't come near us again.'

Angered by what her sister has done and with the worry about the safety of her pup, she seeks out another place to live.

The new den is in a territory where there are a lot of other wolves with a pup. All the mother wolves are there after losing the father of their pup from either being shot dead by humans, becoming sick and dying from the environment, or, as some say, being robbed of their spirit by the spirit witch of the forest.

She feels this would also be ideal for getting to know others in the same situation as her, but it seems a lot of them want to keep to themselves.

Her focus is to take care of Alfa Noon, and every day, she is amazed by the little things he does. Surprised by his antics, she laughs, but she feels lonely for both and wonders if things will always be this way.

Haunted

Chapter 11

Although she hasn't had anything to do with her sister Morana for some time after moving from her previous den, her aunt and father inform her they are helping Morana get a new home near where she lives.

This news confuses Kirakee, and her thoughts are filled with dread. *'Oh no, does this mean trouble again? I really didn't want to live anywhere near her.'*

Feeling doubtful about the situation knowing how Morana will stir up friction for her with the other wolves and cause her to become isolated, she makes a hasty decision to move out of the territory and once again start over again.

News arrives from Kirakee's aunt. 'I've got some bad news, and there isn't any easy way to tell you this, but Dasher is dead.'

Kirakee's legs collapse from under her, and she falls to the ground. 'Gasp...No, no, Dasher is dead. No! I don't want to believe it. How could he die?' she sobs.

'He stopped eating, and because he was already ill for a long time, he just gave up,' her aunt replies.

Eventually, the shock sets in, and she sits thinking about all the things her brother must have been feeling and thinking. He must have been lonely and struggled with everything. He probably thought no one cared.

She realizes how she did not even show she cared by at least seeing him. The guilt and grief she feels. She begins to howl and sob.

She had always hoped that Dasher would turn up one day, and she would see him well and normal again. She just never expected that he would die a sad and lonely death. He did not even know he had nieces and nephews.

A few days later, a visit would lift her spirit. Unexpectedly, Mist arrives to see Alfa Noon once again. Kirakee is not prepared for his arrival, and she has been feeling rather unwell.

'Hello, Mist. This is a surprise. I didn't expect you.'

'Yeah, I thought I'd just drop in to see how the little fellow is going. Is he okay?'

She musters up a smile. 'Yes, he is well. I'm the one not feeling well now, but you can spend some time with him anyway.'

Once again, she is thinking to ask him those questions that have been nagging her thoughts.

'Wait! Let him spend some time with Alfa Noon, and then ask him,' she thinks.

But to her disappointment, within minutes, Mist walks out to the den entrance and announces he is leaving.

She thinks about how strange his visit seemed to be.

She is happy Mist has seen his son again but just cannot understand why he does not see him more often.

Alfa Noon has grown so much more since the last time Mist came to visit. The whole thing bothers her. Why has it turned out this way?

As weeks pass by, Morana makes a point of informing Kirakee that she and a few of her friends have seen Mist out in the forest.

'We followed him for a while when he was with his friends and teased him. I bet he felt a bit stupid,' Morana smugly says.

Kirakee's heart sinks. She is horrified that her sister would do such a thing to Mist and is worried about what Mist must think. Morana is only making things worse. Mist must have been embarrassed being bullied in front of his friends.

'He is going to blame me for Morana bullying him. He is going to think I had something to do with it. Now he probably hates me.'

Kirakee stares at Morana in silence while she is fighting to hold back showing any signs of sadness. She is confused as to why Morana would do such a thing. Is she really thinking about Kirakee's and Alfa Noon's best interests?

Not wanting to create a scene with her sister, she silently walks away with her head hanging down.

Her sister continues laughing and bragging about her bullying Mist. 'It was funny. His friends didn't know what to say either,' Morana chuckles.

Feeling disgusted with her sister's behaviour, she hangs on to the hope of speaking to Mist sometime soon so she can tell him the truth.

'I didn't have anything to do with that,' she whispers to herself.

Often, sadness overwhelms her, and on her sad days when the moon is full, she goes up to the hill she has been to so many times before and howls—wishing for better things to come.

She smiles with delight as she watches her beautiful son teeter up the rocks on the hill, naming every plant he passes.

'You named all of the plants,' she cries out proudly. 'You're a bright little son!'

But as Alfa Noon turns his tiny face to look at her, she feels a twinge of sadness.

'If only your father could be here to see this,' she thinks. 'I know!' she coos while snuggling close to Alfa Noon.

'Why don't I send a wolf messenger to tell Mist about all the little milestones you are making?' she says.

Kirakee decides this would be the only way she could encourage Mist to not give up on them.

In the following days, she waits eagerly for a reply but begins to lose hope after a couple of weeks. She has not heard anything from the wolf messenger.

'Maybe Mist didn't receive the message,' she sadly thinks. *'Or maybe he's moved away?'*

But try as she might to put Mist out of her mind, she just cannot help thinking about him.

A few weeks later, she encounters Morana in the woods while scavenging for food. Their encounter goes well, and Morana is being friendly more than usual.

'You should join us for the spring wolf gathering.'

Kirakee feels a little shocked that her sister would bother to invite her.

Feeling cautious, she declines the invite.

She shakes her head, 'I think I shouldn't.'

Morana looks annoyed and stares in silence for a moment. 'But why wouldn't you want to come to such an event. Have you lost your mind?'

'No! I just need some time to think it over, really.'

Kirakee begins to feel she might be missing out on something if she does not go to the gathering. Secretly she hopes she might run into Mist.

She takes a deep breath and straightens up. 'Okay, I'll go to the gathering then.'

Without another word, they begin their journey to the event.

'He might be here,' she thinks as they enter amongst the wolf gathering. *'After all, this is where all the wolves gather from all around.'*

As she heads to the other side of the gathering, she catches sight of a dark-eyed young wolf with three she-wolves surrounding him.

'He looks okay,' she thinks as he looks and smiles at her. *'But his dirty coat is horrible!'* she thinks.

However, she can see he is not terribly interested in the other wolves with him as he continues to keep his eyes on her. Kirakee blushes a little but then continues, determined to find Mist.

Shortly after arriving, they receive word of another wolf gathering and decide to visit the other. Instantly upon arrival, she finds Mist with some of his friends.

She has not seen him for a couple of months. She informs Morana that she is going to go over and speak to Mist.

'Wish me luck,' she says to Morana.

She walks up to Mist.

'Hello, Mist. Did you get my message from the wolf messenger about Alfa Noon?'

Mist looks at her blankly. 'Yes,' he replies.

'And are you planning to visit?' Kirakee asks.

'No, I'm too busy,' Mist growls.

Kirakee turns away and struggles to hide her sadness; her heart is breaking. *That's it then; it's over. He isn't even interested in giving us any time,'* she thinks.

As she reviews what has happened, she realizes she has been set free. 'It's time to move on now,' she quietly whispers to herself.

She walks back over to Morana.

'He doesn't want anything to do with me,' she says to Morana.

Morana does not express any sympathy for Kirakee's situation, but she seems too pleased.

It is all part of the new plan Morana and her mother have devised. This time, they believe it would be best to keep Kirakee away from Mist and not encourage her to relocate to another territory because it might cause the two territories to unite and provide the time Kirakee needs to grow stronger. This new plan is to keep Kirakee where they can watch over her so they can keep her in a state they have been manipulating for many seasons.

Kirakee shakes her head in disbelief at how cold and uncaring Morana can be, but she knows there is not a thing she can do to change any of the problems; therefore, she reluctantly follows Morana into the woods once again.

Second Chances

Chapter
12

As the spring season is closing to its end, she acknowledges the harshness of what lays ahead for her and Alfa Noon once they pass through the next couple of seasons. The outlook does not look good, as the snow season will create many struggles for survival.

'I wish we had someone to share this with,' she sadly says to Alfa Noon as he plays. 'It's hard being on our own. What if we're alone together every day, forever?'

Later that day, Morana tells her of another wolf gathering to end the season.

'Are we going back to the same location we went to last time?' Kirakee asks with a gleaming smile.

'Yes! Why do you ask? Does it really matter?' Morana says with a frown.

Kirakee shakes her head. 'No! No! It doesn't matter,' she says nervously as she tries to conceal any enthusiasm.

They arrive at the gathering just before midnight and find a rocky spot to sit that gives them a full view of their surroundings.

'This is great,' Kirakee smiles happily.

Suddenly she notices a handsome wolf walking by, and he catches her eye and smiles.

'He's nice!' she thinks.

Her heart skips a beat as she gazes at his brown fur and dark eyes.

'Look at him, Kirakee,' Morana whispers. 'He smiled at you when he walked past!'

'I wonder where he's going. I hope he comes back!' says Kirakee.

A few minutes later, the mysterious wolf comes back, and now he is standing before Kirakee.

'Hi,' he smiles. 'I'm 'Mud.' Would you mind if I sit with you?'

Soon they were chatting happily.

'I was going to a wolf gathering in another location, but my friends decided to not go. So, I thought I'd come out over this way instead,' Mud says.

By the end of the night, she feels as if she has known Mud for years and is pleased when he asks if they can see each other again.

The very next day, he arrives at her den when Alfa Noon is having a nap.

Mud notices him sleeping in the back of the den. 'I didn't know you had a pup. Is it a boy?'

Kirakee blushes. 'Yes. His name is Alfa Noon,' she says with a smile.

'He certainly is a cute little fella,' Mud whispers.

Soon Mud and Kirakee are seeing each other every day, and they find they have a lot in common. Both have had a very tough year with losing a loved one, including the loss of partners.

About a week later, Mud begins talking about the night they first met.

'Before I went out, I took a bath in the stream to wash off a lot of mud that had dried on my coat from a time when I'd become trapped in a mudslide.'

Kirakee stares at him. 'You were covered in mud?' she asks.

Suddenly it clicks with her. Mud is the muddy wolf she had seen one night at one of the gatherings. Kirakee could not believe it!

'You look so different,' she laughs in surprise.

But not only is she and Mud getting on well, Alfa Noon likes him too.

Just within days after they have met, Mud suggests, 'I reckon I should move in with you and Alfa Noon, and you and I start a family.'

'Yeah,' she jokes in response to Mud's suggestion. 'We should start a family?'

'Yes, I'm serious,' Mud says.

A few days later, Mud begins living with Kirakee and Alfa Noon.

Shortly after, she gives birth to three more pups. This time it is a surprise to all the wolves in the territories, for no one has been able to give birth to three surviving pups for a very long time.

It was a long and difficult birth. Kirakee is much older now than the usual wolves breeding years. This most likely will be her last litter of pups.

The firstborn of the litter is 'Night,' and the name is fitting because he was born during the night. Then 'Lunar,' who was born just when a Lunar eclipse occurred that night. And last of all, 'Omega Sunset,' it was almost another day before she entered the world. She calls her Omega because she considers her the last pup she will ever have, and Sunset, as she was born as the sun went down.

Kirakee is so happy. She feels meeting Mud is one of the best things that has ever happened to her. She often thinks about what it all means for her. *'He has restored my faith in finding someone who cares and who loves Alfa Noon as his own. We are soul mates.'*

She has her best friend and soul mate and four pups with her every day. She spends a lot of time taking care of her family and teaching them to fish, hunt, and all they need to know about their surroundings and dangers.

On the nights of the full moon, she takes her pups up to the top of the hill she has visited so many times before and teaches them how to howl at the full moon.

Life feels good. She has her own little family pack and does not need to care about what Morana and the rest of her family are doing now.

Morana visits occasionally. They are good for a while and then, as usual, have their fallouts, but one day, Morana mentions Mist, and Kirakee is intent to talk about him. In a way, Kirakee mistakenly believes she could openly speak about things to Morana.

'You know, I can't help it, but I still have strong feelings for Mist,' Kirakee says.

'What? How can you still have feelings for Mist when you are with Mud,' Morana snaps.

Kirakee feels her sister does not understand her purpose of saying how she feels. 'Well, I never stopped feeling for him. I don't think there is anything wrong with that!'

'Yes, there is. You can't say you still have feelings for Mist and be with Mud at the same time. I'm going to tell Mud,' Morana snaps.

'Why would you do that? I only said I have feelings for him. It doesn't mean I don't have the same for Mud. In fact, I am growing a stronger connection to Mud more as time goes on but having feelings for Mist doesn't mean I can't have them for Mud any more than I do!'

'I'm going to tell Mud. He should know about how you feel,' Morana snaps.

As Morana is leaving, Kirakee is angry with her sister.

'Morana, just stop what you are going to do. It's just going to cause trouble.'

'No, I'm going to tell him. He needs to know,' Morana smugly says as she walks away.

Over the next couple of days, Morana continues to turn up at Kirakee's den, hoping to see Mud so she can tell him what she knows. Kirakee fights with her sister, forcing her to leave.

'Don't come back here. You are not welcome; you're a troublemaker.'

Once again, Kirakee and Morana stop talking again, and since Mud and Kirakee still live in the same territory as Morana, the other wolves stop talking to her as well because Morana spreads rumours about her.

Kirakee feels her happiness is threatened by her sister, so she needs to find another place to live.

Eventually, they move into another territory where the other territory packs accept their presence. Peace befalls upon their family once again.

Life is hectic, and on some days, Kirakee feels exhausted. She has lost a lot of the full confidence she had found after her return from the Orphaned River, and although she does her best to be involved in her pups' active lives, she still feels unsure about her ability.

Her nerves get the better of her sometimes, hence, draining her of energy. But she continues to love and nurture the additional part of her life, living and breathing for them, giving them all her time, watching them grow, and memorizing every milestone.

Her pups entertain her every day. Alfa Noon is wise beyond his years. He is always polite and cooperative, confident, and an active pup.

Zooming past her on a hillside, he goes sledging down on the snow.

'Be careful, Alfa Noon,' she calls out. Then suddenly, a vision quickly invades her mind. *'He is going to be alright. One day he is going to be something special.'*

She smiles as she feels sure she has just had a glimpse of her beautiful son's future life.

As for her other pups, Night, Lunar, and Omega Sunset, they are all different in their own way.

Night has been a lot of hard work. He has become ill quite often. When he is well, he is always getting up to mischief. He is often uncooperative and becomes easily angry, fighting with his brother and sisters and arguing with Kirakee and Mud. This is a concern to Kirakee. She does worry about where all these moods are going to lead him. She has even found that Night is not very affectionate because every time she has tried to snuggle close to him and show him affection, he pushes her away.

Lunar is very quiet. She is more of a listener and a thinker and does not say a lot. She has a squeaky voice compared to her siblings, which makes Kirakee feel drawn to her, as she finds her squeaky voice to be endearing. One problem that does seem to be growing is a rivalry problem between Lunar and Omega Sunset.

Lunar does not have much patience with Omega Sunset and, at times, can be quite aggressive and rough with her sister.

Omega Sunset is a sensitive soul. She is caring and affectionate, but she does worry a lot which does cause her to become rather anxious at times. She is the kind of wolf Kirakee feels will grow to be a kind and generous wolf.

'Mother, do we have to wait until the full moon to visit the hills?' Omega Sunset asks.

Kirakee looks down at her tiny little face and smiles. 'No, we can go to the hills at any time. We can even go today.'

Omega Sunset excitedly jumps around. 'Yay! I love the view from the hills.' She runs off to tell Alfa Noon, Night, and Lunar. 'Quick, quick! Mother is taking us up to the hills. Come on. Let's go!'

They all run for the hills.

'I bet I can get there before you, Alfa Noon,' says Lunar.

'Ha, you think. We will see!' Alfa Noon chuckles.

Alfa Noon arrives at the top of the hill first, with Lunar closely in pursuit.

'Sigh! Alfa Noon, you always win at everything,' Lunar pants.

'Hey, you guys. Stick close together, and keep a lookout for any danger,' says Kirakee.

Everything is clear; the sun is shining. Kirakee's pups continue cheerfully playing together while Kirakee watches over them, but she feels they are being watched. She catches an image in the side of her vision and quickly turns her head to see.

'Who is that?' she thinks.

Just as she stands to her feet and plans to go closer to get a better vision of who the wolf could be, he walks away until he disappears. Considering there is no threat, she continues with her pups on the hill.

They all decide to make a trip to the hills as a daily outing while the weather is good.

She sits and watches her pups playing under the midday sun, and once again, she catches the same image in the corner of her vision.

She quickly stands up and looks straight at the wolf.

He stares back.

She can now see who this mysterious wolf is. 'Mist,' she whispers.

She barely recognizes him. He has matured into a big striking Alpha wolf.

She begins to move forward towards him, hoping he will not disappear. She is thinking about what she could say if she gets to talk to him.

She nervously takes a deep breath and calls out to him. 'Hey, Mist, I nearly...' her voice breaks and sounds squeaky. She clears her throat. 'I nearly didn't recognize you.'

He wags his tail. 'I heard you were up here with Alfa Noon and your other pups and wanted to see how he looked.'

'I think Alfa Noon would like to meet you. Will you stay for a while longer? I'll go and get him,' Kirakee says with a smile.

Without needing to collect Alfa Noon, he has curiously approached, and he exchanges greetings with Mist.

Kirakee wags her tail. 'This is Mist, your father.'

Alfa Noon is surprised and smiles. 'You are different looking than I imagined.'

'Actually, I think you and Mist look rather alike,' Kirakee smiles.

Night, Lunar and Omega Sunset are calling out to Alfa Noon to play, and he has become a little shy, not knowing what to say to Mist.

'I better see what they want,' Alfa Noon says.

Kirakee and Mist use the time to learn about what each has been doing. Mist informs Kirakee of his father's death.

'I'm so sorry, Mist, I didn't know. Did he die of illness?'

'Yes, and after his death, I was alone for a while. The rest of the pack didn't do much to help me or my mother. I felt bad that he never got to know he had a grandson either,' he sadly says.

Kirakee sees the sadness in Mist's face; she hangs her head feeling sad too.

She puts her head up and looks Mist straight in the eye. 'I'm glad you've been able to see Alfa Noon. I didn't think we would ever see you again.'

Thinking this is the moment for her to speak properly to Mist and ask him questions, she takes a deep breath and thinks, *'This is the time. I must ask him everything right now.'*

'There are some things I have never been able to talk to you about, and I'd really like to ask you about a few things that happened a long time ago,' she says nervously.

'Okay, what do you want to know?' Mist asks.

Kirakee takes a deep breath. 'I've always wanted to ask you about....'

Before she can finish her sentence, they hear a deep growl behind them. She looks over her shoulder and quickly jumps up and turns around.

'Gasp! Hi, Mud, what are you doing here,' she says with a startled voice.

Mud is not happy. He disapproves of Mist turning up to see his son after not bothering to have anything to do with him for such a long time.

Mist is uncomfortable with Mud's confrontation and is fidgeting around. 'Look, Mud, I don't want any trouble, and I certainly don't want to bring any trouble to Alfa Noon. So, I'll get out of your way.'

Mist walks away.

Kirakee takes a few steps forward and calls out to Mist. 'I'm sorry,

Mist, please don't feel bad. You haven't done anything wrong with coming to see Alfa Noon.'

Mist stops, turns around, and looks at Kirakee. 'Don't worry about it. I don't want to upset Alfa Noon and his family. He would be better off if I keep out of things. You continue taking care of the boy. You've done a good job. He is a fine young wolf.'

Kirakee just wants to sit there and howl, but she cannot because Mud is still nearby. She collects her pups and returns home.

Mud does not say anything else about Mist, and Kirakee decides it would be best to stay silent about what she feels about Mud's approach to Mist.

Suspicious Behaviour

Chapter 13

Kirakee attempts to rekindle a relationship with her own father once again after a previous fallout brought on by her sister Morana lying to their father about the purpose of an argument between her sister and her. But Mud is unsure of her intentions and does not support her visiting her father. He has seen how Kirakee's father tends to lean on Morana's side every time there is trouble between the two sisters.

Their father has expressed his distaste for Kirakee by not bothering to associate with her family pack, and her sons have seen him at Morana's den quite often, which in turn has caused them some heartache.

One day, Kirakee's father criticizes her, claiming she has started all the trouble between her and her sister.

'I think you need to get your head fixed, Kirakee,' her father says.

Kirakee is upset by her father blaming her mental state for the reason of her own sister's bad behaviour.

'That's not fair, father. She is a troublemaker. She tells lies and has twisted the facts by putting the blame on me. I've tried with her so many times, and she has done many things to show she doesn't care.'

'Well, she has told me different stories, and it would seem you have a problem. Not her,' he says angrily.

Mud is listening to the conversation, and he becomes enraged. 'Listen here, old wolf, if you are going to be like that, then don't expect us to return any support we owe you.'

Kirakee's father is shocked and enraged. 'Well, don't you bother.' He angrily walks away.

'Don't worry about them, Kirakee. Your sister is nothing but trouble, and your father is a silly old wolf,' Mud says.

She is so glad she is not the only one who can see the problems she has encountered with her sister, and now Mud is along by her side with him understanding. This is comforting.

But something has clicked within Kirakee. Her mother being presumed dead, and her brother's death constantly plague her thoughts. She realizes there are so many other things that can be done for the better of others instead of being bogged down in constant battles with her family members.

She feels a strong urge to do something about the wolves that need help. Within a few days, she begins to seek out the wolves who have been abandoned, knowing many of them are depressed.

She sits and talks to them, listens to their stories, and then goes about her territory speaking to the many other packs, seeking their support to raise awareness about the problems the lost wolves are encountering.

She feels the need to do so much more to help them, but her plea for help for the lost and scattered wolves is met with negativity from the packs, as the Kingdom of the wolves has become faint out of fear because of the new invasion of mankind.

The wolves believe discarding or leaving the weaker members behind or excluding them from the packs will make the wolf packs appear much stronger.

She can see there is so much work to do for her to be able to convince the packs to think otherwise, but at this time, her own family pack keep her busy, and she needs so much more time to make her mission work.

After a long and happy union, cracks are beginning to show between Kirakee and Mud.

'Poor little Alfa Noon,' Mud sarcastically says to Kirakee.

Kirakee has always openly maintained her bond with Alfa Noon and has never felt uncomfortable showing her affection towards him. But Mud is now showing some jealousy towards them because of the attention she shows her son. This is making her feel uncomfortable, and she does not want Alfa Noon to hear these comments.

The only thing she can do to protect Alfa Noon is to refrain from showering him with affection when Mud is around. But as Alfa Noon has become old enough to participate in territory activities, she makes sure she is there to watch and support him with whatever he is doing. She is determined to not let Mud make her feel uncomfortable for doing that.

Mud is increasingly showing more of his bad temper and taking it out on his family by throwing violent temper tantrums. He is belittling Kirakee increasingly more as each new day passes.

'You are a stupid, useless she-wolf. Can't you do anything right?' he angrily says to Kirakee in front of their sons because she is unable to break up a fight between Alfa Noon and Night.

Her sons have grown a lot bigger than her, and it is impossible for her to stop them from fighting. It frustrates Kirakee that Mud would speak like that to her quite often in front of their offspring. She does not want her sons to think they can treat their own kind like this or to think it is okay to look down on anyone when they are struggling.

Mud and Kirakee are arguing a great deal now over many things. Mud is hardly ever home as he is always out with other wolves. He has always been extremely competitive, and because of his bad temper, he often becomes involved in pack brawls.

Kirakee has tried many times to calm him down and talk him through his bad temper in the hope that he will become more passive, but Mud just does not seem happy anymore. He is more concerned with his own interests rather than doing things with his own family.

Another big concern for Kirakee is that she has found out he is a thief. He steals from the other packs in the territory, even from his own family. She recalls what happened to Cloud's partner when he was caught stealing. He was banished from the territory. She is worried this is going to happen to her own family.

No matter what Kirakee says to him about what is wrong, he becomes more critical of her.

'Why don't you get off your backside and go out and do some work instead of sitting around here all day,' he angrily says.

Kirakee feels sick upon hearing his words. 'You obviously haven't been here enough to take notice of all the things I have been doing for our pups every day,' she growls.

The tension continues to escalate between her and Mud. She wants to pacify the situation in any way she can; therefore, she visits the Legend wolf pack. She believes Mud may be suffering from more than just dissatisfaction with Kirakee and suspects the environment may be affecting him.

While seeking advice from the Legends' pack, she expresses she would like to help other wolves too who are suffering from mental health problems.

Although her intentions are honorable, the Legends pack do not believe she is currently ready to take on so much responsibility with their knowledge.

'You're still a bit young Kirakee to be obtaining this knowledge.'

'Why am I too young. I'm much older than the wolves with pups. I don't think I'm too young, really. Besides, I've come to understand a lot from loss and from my own struggles. I'm probably much wiser than most of the other wolves in our territories,' she replies.

The Legend wolves privately discuss Kirakee's situation, and after a great deal of debating amongst their members, they accept Kirakee's request.

'Okay, come back here tomorrow, and you'll need to return here every day until we know you have learnt enough.'

Kirakee is thrilled.

She runs home, excited to share the news with her family.

After instructing her family she will need their support and cooperation for her to spend time with the Legend pack, she makes sure that everything is organized every day for her pups while she spends each day away.

The Rise and Decline

Chapter
14

Kirakee receives some very surprising news. She learns her brother Dasher had a pup long before he went missing. When she meets Dasher's son Jasp, she is surprised at how he is so much of a chip off the old block.

She learns Jasp is frail like her brother and believes she can help him. Jasp struggles with confidence. Jasp and Kirakee build a strong bond and he begins to become a solid member of her pack.

Mud and Alfa Noon are heading out on a wolf gathering and have invited Jasp. Kirakee encourages Jasp to accompany them and hopes Mud will watch out for him as Jasp does not usually socialize.

Jasp is met with a difficult situation when he is bullied by a few of Mud's company and with Mud being so occupied with his own popularity, he does not attend to Jasp to put an end to the problem.

Jasp tries to find his way home and comes upon a den and is mistaken to be a thief by a pack of wolves who occupy the territory. He is chased out of the territory.

Kirakee does not hear from Jasp for a few days leaving her to believe he has found something else to do while she studies with the Legend pack.

Upon her arrival home from the Legend territory, she is met with bad news from Mud that Jasp had been driven into a dangerous situation and has lost his life.

Kirakee is distraught.

She visits the Legends pack and expresses her grief as well as her resentment towards Mud for not supervising Jasp well enough. She also blames herself for sending Jasp off into a less than wholesome social situation, so she decides to stop her studies with the Legends until she returns to a better frame of mind.

Mud and Kirakee completely fall apart. Kirakee asks Mud to not be in the same den for a while, so Mud leaves without a protest.

Within a few weeks, he hooks up with a much younger she-wolf with a young pup she birthed from another territory pack.

Kirakee protests about Mud's latest union, and her son Night becomes more critical of Kirakee, blaming her for his father leaving. Kirakee is troubled by Night's anger towards her.

Kirakee seeks advice from the Legends pack to help her understand what the best thing is for her to do with Mud. They suggest a meeting with both Mud and Kirakee. They believe they can provide them with enough information to encourage them to rebuild their alliance for their own pack.

Mud agrees to attend and agrees to try and be with his family again. But after a couple of days, the young she-wolf, named Pit, comes calling on Kirakee, demanding answers to why Kirakee thinks she is worth any less than her since she had expressed, she did not want Mud around in the first place.

Kirakee tries to smooth things over for the young she-wolf but is to find Pit is determined to get Mud back as she threatens to put herself in harm's way. Mud cracks and returns to Pit.

The pups are now moving between two dens, but they are not happy with their situation with Pit being there with her young pup.

Kirakee tries to change the situation, so her own pups are with her more often, but Mud refuses to change the arrangement. So, Kirakee makes sure to enhance her time with her pups by sharing extra special moments with them so they will never feel like they are missing out on anything. One of the activities the pups take delight in is dancing on the hills under the northern lights. Kirakee promises them she will always make sure this activity is their special time with her.

It has been a few seasons since Kirakee has seen her father and sister Morana. Kirakee receives news of her father's health from one of her old wolf clan members. Her father is gravely ill, so she sets out to make peace with him.

Upon her visit, Morana shows up, and her father's attention is consumed by Morana's presence. Kirakee leaves, and upon her departure, she tells her father she will keep in touch and see him again.

For the next couple of weeks, Kirakee continues to visit her father with her pups, but Morana is always present.

Morana makes it her mission to charm herself into the company of Kirakee's daughters by inviting them to her home den, but Kirakee is obligated to accompany her daughters on their visit and is put in an awkward situation of having to be around her sister.

Her son Night chooses to spend more time with his father, Mud and is not interested in Morana's company, and Morana knows it.

Alfa Noon has also been spending a great deal more time with Night, and he has also expressed his opinion about Morana. His opinion is beginning to rub off onto his little brother.

During the visit, Kirakee's daughters take a shine to Morana and insist on being a part of her company more often. Morana frequently criticizes Kirakee in front of her daughters, leaving her daughters to question Kirakee as to why their aunt says degrading things to her.

Kirakee declines to tell them the whole story since they are too young to comprehend all.

Morana makes sarcastic remarks about Kirakee's departure from Mud and blames Kirakee for the breakdown of their relationship. She claims she knows more about Kirakee's life activities than what Kirakee would have expected her to know since they have not been socializing for a few seasons.

Kirakee is not sure of how to handle the situation with Morana and the time her daughters are spending with their aunt. Kirakee is beginning to feel like they are being trapped.

During the time her pups are not with her, she sets about visiting other wolf packs in her territory to talk to the elders about the depressed wolves and other health issues in their territory, but she is finding she is getting nowhere with making them understand the need to help the frail and sick pack members.

Instead, the elders have made their minds up and inform Kirakee that they are too busy avoiding the threat of man to be slowed down by what they consider the weak. They also believe Kirakee is not wise enough to be counselling them over such issues; therefore, they chase her out of their territory.

Meanwhile, on her own home front, she finds Morana showing her displeasure for the work she is doing. Morana criticizes every aspect of Kirakee's good intentions.

It is time to farewell Alfa Noon. He has grown into a handsome, strong, and wise wolf. Now he is old enough to explore his options, and of recent times, he has befriended a pack in another territory. After spending a great deal of time with the new pack, he is accepted as one of the Alpha leaders of the territory.

With the speedy change taking place within Kirakee's own family pack, she attempts to rebuild her relationship with her younger son, Night. A new wolf gathering provides Kirakee with the opportunity to spend more time with him.

Her son's outlook is maturing. This new outlook is helping Kirakee and Night to speak civilly, but she finds Night still very protective of his father, Mud.

She chooses her words carefully when they discuss anything about his father.

Little by little, she is beginning to put all of what is left of her family back together, so she thinks.

Light and Darkness

Chapter 15

With the arrival of spring, the birds are singing, going about their early morning chore of gathering food to feed their babies and build their nests.

Kirakee smiles and jumps around in the tall grass as if to dance to the whistles of the birds. But something is lurking in the nearby woods. Crackling and rustling capture her attention. She stands still and peers towards the woods, attempting to focus as the sunlight blinds her vision.

Determined to gain a clear view, she begins to walk closer to the forest tree line.

The sun is no longer blinding her, the clouds above become an eerie kind of darkness.

The birds stop singing, and in the darkness of the eerie sky, the predatory birds circle just like they do when there is death.

Suddenly before her appears a dark shadow of a figure clinging to the top of a tree.

'Hello! Who goes there? Who are you?'

The dark and mysterious figure begins to slither down from the treetop, then stops and stares at Kirakee.

'Gasp! Who are you?' Kirakee nervously asks.

Amongst the intense smoky darkness, red ruby eyes peer back at her. There is an eerie silence.

Kirakee shudders. There is an intense heat being emitted from the figure, and it causes her fur to cling closely to her body.

Kirakee's heart races. She begins to pant rapidly but doesn't show her fear. She straightens up and takes a deep breath, and then takes another step forward, but before she can move forward any further, the mysterious creature slithers back up the tree like floating smoke, then floats away, back over the treetops until it disappears into the depths of the forest.

Kirakee takes another deep breath and exhales. 'What the heck was that?' she whispers as she shakes her head in disbelief.

Alarmed by her encounter and the feeling that all is not safe, she feels the urgency to gather her pups and protect them.

Straight away, she heads to Morana's to pick up her daughters in case they are still there before they are meant to head over to their father's den to reunite with Night.

After briskly making her way to Morana's den, she finds her daughters have already departed.

She warns Morana of what she has encountered and expresses her fear of danger. However, Morana discredits Kirakee and claims Kirakee is just making things up and exaggerating.

An argument pursues. Kirakee questions everything about Morana's motives and protests about her criticism of her. Morana claims Kirakee twists everything around, and this frustrates Kirakee further.

As Kirakee is leaving, she tells Morana she should never have bothered with her and tells her to keep away from her and her family.

A couple of days later, Night, Lunar and Omega Sunset return home to Kirakee's den from Mud's place. The first thing they greet her with is distressing news.

'Mother, Aunty Morana said you and her had an

argument.' 'When did she tell you that?' Kirakee asks

'She came and picked us up from fathers' den yesterday and took us out on an outing. She said you came into her place and started an argument, and you were snapping like a mad wolf,' says Lunar.

Kirakee is angered by the news. 'Oh, did she now. Well, that's a lie. She started an argument by criticizing me, and I wasn't snapping like a crazy wolf.'

Thoughts are running through her head. *How dare she tell a lie to my own pups to discredit me. Now she is interfering with my family even after telling her to keep away. She is now tampering with my relationship with my own offspring. I must stop her before she ruins everything.'*

She realizes there and then how Morana has and will always walk all over her, and she needs to fight back more than she has ever done before.

'I'm going to talk to your father as well about this. Your aunt is a troublemaker, and we need to keep her away from us,' Kirakee angrily says.

The next day, she heads towards Mud's den, and as usual, the birds are happily going about their business, and the forest is alive.

Just as she is about to reach Mud's den, once again, an eerie silence befalls upon the forest.

'Gasp!' She looks around but doesn't see any danger, but she senses she is not alone.

Not feeling comfortable, she speeds up her pace.

Just as she passes a rocky hill, she feels the ground rumble below her feet. The sound of thunder deafens her. She looks up and catches a glimpse of a large boulder rock speeding down the hill towards her.

With a startling leap, she turns around and begins to run. Smaller rocks speed past her, but she is not fast enough to outrun the largest rock of them all.

The boulder hits her with the power of nothing she has felt before. She is flattened to the ground and completely knocked out unconscious.

Complete darkness is all that exists, but within seconds in her unconscious state, she begins to hear the faint sound of beeps, then voices, but they are human voices. The voices sound stressed.

'Code Blue.'

'Hurry, get the doctor. She is convulsing.'

'Clear the way. We are losing her.'

'Quick, hand me the defibrillator.'

In the darkness, a pin of light begins to grow bigger until there is a brilliant golden glowing light.

The faint figure of a human's face begins to appear.

'Kirakee!' the voice gently whispers.

Kirakee gasps, 'How do you know my name?'

'It's me, Kira.'

'Kira? I know your name. I've heard it before, but how do we know each other's names?'

'I'm not sure, but I think we are connected.'

'How are we connected?'

'I'm not sure, but I think it has something to do with our mothers.'

'How is this possible?' Kirakee asks.

'I don't know exactly, but I know you are in great danger.'

'How am I in danger?'

'Don't trust anyone. There are evil forces surrounding you.'

Kirakee gasps. 'How do you know this?'

'I see we are connected. You must be stronger and drink the water of the Orphaned River.'

'No, that's forbidden.'

'You are being deceived, Kirakee. Good will happen when you drink of the Orphaned River. You will see things clearly. Just don't emerge your body in the water. It's not safe for you.'

'How do you know these things? Where are you?'

'I can't stay; I've got to go. Be stronger, Kirakee.'

'Where are you going?' Kirakee shouts.

Before Kirakee can gain the answers to her questions, the light begins to fade, and so does Kira's face disappear back into the darkness. The faint sound of human voices and beeping dominate the darkness once again.

'We have her back.'

'Watch her closely for the next 24 hours and make sure she is comfortable.'

She begins to hear another voice.

'Kirakee, Kirakee, wake up!'

She begins to slowly open her eyes. Her vision is blurry. She continuously blinks.

'Kirakee, wake up! It's me, Tick Tock.'

She turns her head, and with a fuzzy vision, she can just see Tick Tock.

She gasps in shock and then slowly sits up.

'What happened?' she says with a weak voice.

Tick Tock moves closer to her. 'You were knocked out by a falling rock.'

Feeling drowsy, she gently shakes her head. 'What? Knocked out?'

Tick Tock nods. 'Yes! Yes! But you are okay now?'

She squints her eyes. Her head hurts. 'Oh, I don't know, Tick Tock. I don't feel so good.'

Her thoughts are hazed, but suddenly her eyes open wide when she remembers.

'Now I remember, I had the strangest dream. It was so very real. A human was talking to me and warned me about danger, and I think she told me to be stronger. She said other things too, but I just can't remember them right now.'

'Well, that's understandable, Kirakee. You've just taken a nasty blow to your head and possibly imagined things while you were unconscious. As for what you were doing beforehand and remembering things, it might take a little while for you to remember everything.'

Kirakee suddenly stands up. She is beginning to remember more. She growls. 'I was on a mission to see Mud about trouble Morana has been stirring up, and then a rockfall. Oh, I bet that sister of mine did this. I wouldn't put it past her.'

Anger begins to consume her and an urgency to complete her mission.

'Tick Tock, I have something important to take care of right now. I must be going. I'll see you again soon.'

Her legs wobble, but she begins to stride through her state.

Tick Tock flutters up into the trees. 'Hoot! Hoot! Take care,' he says. However, he flies above Kirakee, watching over her to make sure she will be okay.

Upon arriving at Mud's, she speaks to Mud about what happened between her and Morana and tells him what they need to do.

'Now you know the truth, we need to keep her away from all of us.'

But Mud disagrees. He believes the problem is only between her and Morana, and no one else needs to be getting involved.

Kirakee warns of Morana's influence on their pups. She does not believe she has good intentions; she believes her aim is to corrupt her wolf pack. But Mud does not listen to reason, and his response is in support of Morana.

Kirakee leaves feeling bewildered. She knows that if she does not stop Morana, the problems with her family will become an even bigger problem.

Over the next couple of days, her daughters reveal to her that Morana has become good friends with their father's new partner, Pit and with Mud. As Kirakee finds out, Morana was not just spending time with her daughters on outings when they were in their father's care, but Morana had become chummy with Pit and Mud long beforehand. This makes sense as to why Mud would choose to be so uncooperative with her because of an alliance they had developed with Morana.

This makes Kirakee mad. She knows Morana will not stop. She knows her so well. Morana will get her teeth into everything to bring it to ruin, but Kirakee feels like she is stuck and quickly sinking in quicksand.

Trapped

Chapter 16

After a couple of days of feeling depressed and stressed, she must step out of her den to gather her pups from their father's den.

The sun is shining, and the birds are chirping. This tends to lift her spirit.

While she walks, she shakes her head, trying to shake off all the feelings that have consumed her for the past few days.

She hears a noise behind her and turns around. It's Morana following her.

Kirakee gasps with shock. 'What are you doing, Morana?'

Morana is now standing right in front of her.

'You're jealous of me,' Morana smugly says

Kirakee shakes her head. 'Why would you say that? I'm disgusted that you have caused trouble once again.'

Morana growls. 'You're the troublemaker. Fancy trying to stop me from seeing the pups. I'm good for them, and Mud and Pit will tell you that. You're just jealous that I have more than you.
I have a big den, I have strong alliances with many wolves around Morakee, a new partner, and many people who admire me. What have you got? You've got nothing,' Morana sarcastically says.

'I don't care what you have, Morana. My main concern is my family pack, but now you are interfering with that. Just like you have done with just about anything I have ever had in my life. Alliances, mates, and now my own family. When will you ever stop?' Kirakee snaps.

'Loser Kirakee. I'm happy, and you are not,' Morana smugly says.

'You're a thief, Morana. You're not going to get away with this.'

Morana walks off laughing.

Kirakee stands frozen and then hangs her head down, shaking it. 'How can she be so wicked?' she whispers.

Kirakee returns to Mud and informs him of Morana's behaviour, but he has become set on his own opinion.

'Go away, Kirakee. You crackpot. You are driving away your own offspring. It's what you're doing. They will work you out more and more as they get older. They already are. They would rather be with me. You're just a sad and lonely wolf. Jealous of what your sister and I have. You have nothing.'

'You just sound like my sister. Two peas in a pod. It's just all about power to both of you. Well, let's just see about that,' she snaps.

Kirakee sees how a much bigger crack has grown in her relationship with her pups.

All of them are becoming defiant and accusing her of the same things Mud, Pit, and Morana are saying about her.

Things are out of control, and Kirakee knows it.

Without Mud's support, things are never going to get any better.

The situation escalates into disaster with Lunar when Kirakee disciplines Lunar for being disrespectful.

Lunar takes off to Mud's den to live on a permanent basis.

Kirakee goes over to Mud's place to try and sort things out with Lunar, but it does not go well when Mud intervenes, and an argument pursues. Omega Sunset does not approve and declares she wants to stay with her father more often too.

Believing she should not settle for the way things have turned out with her family, she decides to visit the Legend pack to see if they can support her. They arrange to have a meeting with Mud and Kirakee together so they can sort things out, but Mud does not turn up.

A week passes, and there is no improvement between Kirakee and her pups. In fact, they are becoming increasingly more distant from her ever than before.

She is also dealing with the wolves in her district talking about her and snubbing her. Rumours are going around about her relationship with her pups, and many are coming to the opinion that she must be a bad mother because her pups would rather be with their father than be with her.

Kirakee feels like all her pride and heart have been ripped out.

As the days pass by, she is distinctly feeling unwelcome in her own territory and begins to struggle to survive. She is without any support from any other members of her family and finds she can't afford to stay where she is living.

No one is sticking by her side. She has turned to her father for help, and he has turned his back on her and turned her away because of Morana.

Arguments break out between her and the other wolves, and now there is no way she can stay in her home den any longer.

A Wise Old Friend

Chapter
17

She is worn out, feeling rejected and defeated. She will have to find another den.

Since she will be leaving the territory, she visits Mud and her pups to tell them of her plans. Lunar, Night, and Omega Sunset do not want to talk to her, so she only speaks to Mud.

Mud does not argue with her but seems to be more pleased than anything else about her news.

She walks away with her head hanging down.

With nowhere to go, she wanders around in the woods for a while. There is a display of the Northern lights, so she heads for the hilltops and lays down on top of the hill, wishing she could just fade away.

'Hey, Kirakee, what are you doing?' asks Tick Tock.

'Tick Tock, it's just not a good time,' she sadly says.

Tick Tock flutters over and sits down close to Kirakee. 'You can't give up; you are needed.'

She turns her head and looks at Tick Tock. 'No, I'm not. My pups don't need me. They'd rather be with their father, and I have nothing left,' she sobs.

'We need you, Kirakee.'

"Who is we?' she asks

'You're a good wolf. Look at the things you have tried to do to help the downtrodden, the sick, the forgotten and rejected.'

'Yeah, and I'm all of those now. I'm just like them,' she sadly says.

Tick Tock attempts to comfort her. 'I'm sorry to say it has gone this way for a reason. You can't give up. More than anything else, you have come to understand the struggles of others because of your own. Only you can understand how much all need your support to get through the hard times.'

'Well, that is true, but I'm too tired to fight for others right now. All my family just want me to disappear, and that's all I feel like doing,' she whimpers.

'I won't argue with that. That is true. Mud, Pit and Morana have only brought you trouble and grief, but it's been out of their own greed and want for power. You are not like that, Kirakee. You are unique, and by giving up, you would be giving Mud, Pit and Morana what they want. They want you to disappear. Don't let them have their way.'

'But how can I get my pups to see and understand this? They are doing everything to please Mud, Pit and Morana, and anything I say gets criticized like I'm the only one at fault.'

Tick Tock jumps onto Kirakee's head and whispers into her ear, 'They will see the truth one day. Trust what I tell you. You are going to do great things.'

'Who me? I don't think so, Tick Tock. I can't even get anything to stay great. Everything has turned out terrible.'

'Trust me, Kirakee. I can't explain everything to you right now, but I can tell you, I know enough about you to know that you can make a difference.'

Kirakee thinks long and hard about everything Tick Tock has said. *' What if my pups need me one day? They will need me to be here. Maybe I could try for a bit longer and see if things will get better.'*

Everything Tick Tock has said cause her to become curious, and she wants to find out, what will happen, but she does feel Tick Tock is holding something back and not revealing all. It does seem like a curious behaviour.

Her curiosity spurs her on. She moves forward with the encouraging words from her wise owl friend.

She is accepted into a wolf pack in a different territory, but she moves away from the territory quite quickly after learning one member has a strange obsession with the existence of the forest witch. And with that information, it makes Kirakee feel unsettled.

Eventually, she finds another spot to make her home. It is a large cave, but she feels it is way too big for her alone. Then she has a thought. *'I can seek out a few of the downtrodden and depressed wolves. I'll be able to help them by giving them some shelter and somewhere to stay.'*

She searches in and around the surrounding territories and gathers several wolves, less than what she had thought she would find.

Her little forest critter friends visit her quite often by hiding in the trees from the other wolves.

Tick Tock keeps her informed of how Stark, Tarkin and Sheena are doing as he flies back and forth from where they are living.

Alfa Noon visits a few times, and she enjoys hearing about his new adventures. However, there is that great sense of loss from not being with her other pups, as well.

She has a plan.

With the next display of the Northern lights, she sends a wolf messenger to her youngest pups to meet her on the hill so they can watch the light show together.

Being sure they would at least be interested in being a part of this event, she waits eagerly at the site. But when her pups arrive, they are with their aunt Morana and completely ignore Kirakee's existence.

Feeling heartbroken to see Morana taking her place and sharing the light show with the pups, it is too much for her to deal with, so she walks away.

Tick Tock is in a tree when she arrives home. 'Hoot, hoot, Kirakee.'

'Hi Tick Tock, it's happening again. I feel betrayed again,' she says sadly.

'I know. I did see what happened,' Tick Tock says.

'Oh really. I didn't see you. Why are they doing this?'

'I think your sister Morana is hell-bent on making your life miserable and taking away your happiness. She has fed on Mud's vulnerability by siding with him to make things worse between you and your family pack.'

'But why, Tick Tock?'

'I believe you are going to find out that sometime very soon, and I'm going to make sure you can count on me to be always by your side.'

'Well, thank you, Tick Tock. I have no doubt you will watch out over me since I know you do that a lot from the treetops,' she giggles.

Once again, she picks up the pieces of what is left of herself and continues to seek out other lost wolves.

She comes across one sitting down on the banks of a stream. She introduces herself and acquires of any other wolf's whereabouts.

The lone wolf looks down. 'I did belong to a pack not that long ago, but they scattered when the threat of man came near our territory, and ever since, I've been alone,' he says with a tone of sadness.

Kirakee puts her head on his shoulder. 'Don't worry. I can help you. I have a den with a few other wolves that have been just like you. Please join us.'

He is happy Kirakee is giving him a place where he can feel like he belongs.

Betrayal and Defeat

Chapter 18

During her search of the nearby forests, she encounters Lunar and Omega Sunset. For the first time, they seem pleased to see her and ask if they can accompany her on her search through the forests.

Kirakee requests that they ask their father and get his permission so there will be no confusion about spending that time with her.

She waits outside Mud's den and wonders, *'Why are they taking so long to come back out?'*

'Kirakee, Kirakee,' says Tuck, the raccoon.

'Hi, Tuck, what is it. Are you okay?'

'Yes, yes, but Tick Tock has sent me to warn you of trouble.'

'Trouble? Where is Tick Tock?' she asks.

'He is on his way. You need to get out of here because Pit has seen you waiting for your daughters, so she has spread a lie about you amongst many of her friends. She has told them; you are sitting outside their den stalking. Now they are heading over here to get you. They are saying they are going to pull you to pieces.'

'Oh, no. She is crazy. Why would she do that to me? Now I know why Lunar and Omega Sunset haven't come out of their father's den.'

Tick Tock arrives and flutters over onto a rock nearby to Kirakee. 'Quickly, quickly! You must leave, Kirakee. They are coming.'

Just as Tick Tock finishes warning her, she can hear the rustling of the nearby bushes becoming louder. The growling within the shrubs is beginning to dominate all other surrounding sounds.

'Gasp! It sounds like there are a lot of them?' she says.

'There are several. You need to run, Kirakee. Run for safety,' Tick Tock stresses.

Kirakee runs, with Tuck closely behind. The pack are now in their sight, running after them.

Kirakee is concerned for Tuck. 'Tuck, run up into the trees. You must get up high for your own safety.'

Tuck runs up into the nearest tree while Kirakee continues to run. She runs as fast as she can until she is finally out of sight.

Puffing and panting, she is exhausted. 'Traitor. Mad wolves. What gives any of them the right to do that to me?' she mumbles.

She stands still and looks back over her shoulder. The sadness completely consumes her. She feels defeated and bewildered by the fact that they have resorted to driving her completely away from her own.

As she approaches her home, one of her new pack members comes running over to her. 'Hey Kirakee, you'll never guess the kind of rumour is going around about you.'

'Oh, what? I hope it's not another bad one I don't already know about. I've had enough bad things happen today,' she mumbles.

'I understand, but I think you better sit down before I tell you about this one.'

Kirakee sits. 'Okay, what is it?'

'I did as you asked. I looked around for any other wolves in need of some help. I found one and offered him to join us. I explained what you are doing to help the downtrodden, but upon hearing your name, he freaked out.'

'Ha, why did he freak out?' she frowns.

'Well, he said he was told about you a few moons ago. He was given directions to where to find you, but it wasn't in this location. He was sent to another part of the forest where a witch lives in the hollow of a large tree. She calls herself Kirakee.'

Kirakee's jaw drops open. 'She calls herself Kirakee? So, what happened? I have heard about a spirit witch in the forest, but not by the same name as me. I was told a story when I was a pup, but thought it was just a story my sister told me to upset me,' she shakes her head in disbelief.

'Well, there is more to the story. As it turns out, he approached a tree where the witch resides, but an elderly owl fluttered down from the tree and told him to quickly leave. The old owl told him he was in great danger if the witch were to see him, and many wolves that have been looking for you, Kirakee, have been sent to the wrong Kirakee, the witch, and then they have perished.'

Kirakee is in shock. She shakes her head, trying to comprehend what this means.

'So, what you are telling me is that other wolves have come to find me, but someone has sent them to the forest witch instead, so they've been deceived on the account of my name?'

'Yes. And many have lost their lives because of it.'

Kirakee jumps to her feet; she is horrified and angered. 'This is outrageous. Who would ever do such a thing? I must go and see this witch for myself and get some answers.'

'Are you sure that's a good idea, Kirakee? It would be dangerous, and how would you ever be able to get close enough to her

156

without putting yourself in harm's way?'

'I don't know now. I'll have to give it some thought and sleep on it for now, but I have an idea of who can help me find out about what's going on. We've got to put a stop to this,' she growls.

Curious Behaviour

Chapter 19

Early the next day, she steps outside of her den to find Tick Tock and Tuck in a nearby tree.

'Hey guys, I need to talk to you. I need a favour,' she says.

Tick Tock flutters down onto a nearby branch close to Kirakee. 'How can we help my friend?'

'I have a big problem. I was told last night by one of my newest guests that there is a witch in the forest that goes by my name, and someone has been sending wolves to her when they have been looking for me. I need you guys to come with me while I go and see her. I need to stop this.'

'Gasp!' I'm sorry, Kirakee, but I can't go with you. I can't help,' says Tick Tock.

'I can, I can,' says Tuck.

'Okay, thanks, Tuck, but I sense there is a problem with you, Tick Tock. You look nervous. Are you okay?'

Tick Tock nervously clears his throat. 'I'm sorry I can't help you, Kirakee. I can't tell you anymore.'

'Okay, there is obviously something wrong, Tick Tock. If you can't, then I'll just go with Tuck, but could we have a chat when I come back?'

'Okay, sure, but I'm not sure whether I'll be able to be here when you return today, but when it's a good time, I'll talk to you about things later.'

Kirakee goes back into the den to see her newest guest. 'Would you please come with me today, so you can show me where this witch is located?'

'I don't mind helping you, Kirakee, but it's not safe,' he replies.

'I understand what you are saying, but I only want you to take us in to the territory of the witch. You don't have to stay once I find her whereabouts. You can leave before that. Are you okay with that?'

'Okay, Kirakee, I can do that,' he nervously says.

As she approaches where the witch resides, Tuck walks alongside her.

'Aren't you nervous, Kirakee? I am.'

'No. Strangely enough, I'm not. I'm just angry, Tuck.'

Upon their arrival at the tree the witch resides in, it is obvious the tree is one of the oldest trees in the forest. Its enormous size dominates the forest floor. At the base is a large hollow opening. It's dark and quiet.

'Hello, is anyone there,' Kirakee calls out.

In the silence, Tuck and Kirakee hear a grunt come from within the hollow.

'Hello, my name is Kirakee of Morakee. Reveal yourself. Why do you have the same name as me and use it to lure strangers into your trap?'

From the hollow, a pair of eyes glow in the dark. 'Go away and leave me alone,' says the witch.

'Oh, you don't sound like you're going to be very cooperative. Well, I'm not leaving until I have answers. Who are you?' Kirakee growls.

'It's none of your business,' says the crooked voice of the witch.

'Yes, it is my business. I've had to put up with my sister calling me a name ever since I was younger because of you, and now you use my name to cause other wolves harm,' she snaps.

Tuck taps Kirakee on the shoulder. 'What name have you been called by your sister?'

Kirakee turns her head and looks down at Tuck. 'Witches poo.'

Tuck's eyes and mouth open wide in shock. 'How rude is that.'

Kirakee nods. 'Yes. I hate it.'

The witch grunts and then clears her throat. 'Well, you need to take that up with your sister. You must have problems.'

'Yes, I do, but you are a problem too. You must stop what you are doing. Stop using my name, so it will stop the unsuspecting wolves from being lured to you. You need to leave the territory, or I'm going to bring the Legend wolf pack back with me to remove you,' Kirakee shouts out.

'No, no. No need to bring the Legends pack into it. Now just go away and leave me alone,' the witch nervously says.

'Well, if you don't stop ruining the wolves, you will be destroyed. Do you hear me?' Kirakee angrily says.

'Okay, okay. Now just go away, and leave me alone,' says the witch.

Kirakee and Tuck turn around and walk away.

'Shrew, glad that one is over,' Tucks says as he walks alongside Kirakee while giving her a pat on the side.

'I hope it is over, Tuck, but if I find out she is still doing the same thing, then she is going to have to deal with a great deal of fury.'

As she approaches her home den, her guests stand outside cheering, jumping up and down, seeing that Kirakee has returned home safely.

'Well done, Kirakee,' Tick Tock says.

'Thank you, Tick Tock.'

Tuck jumps up. 'Wish you could have been there when she spoke to that witch. You would have been proud of how she handled everything.'

'No need for me to have been there for me to be proud of you. I've always felt proud of you ever since we began being friends,' Tick Tock says with a smile.

'Oh, really, Tick Tock? I'm humbled. But I can't help thinking that it all seemed to be so easy with the witch,' she frowns.

'Yeah, I thought that too. That witch sounded a bit nervous. It all seemed a bit strange,' says Tuck.

Over the next week, several more downtrodden wolves are found and join Kirakee's den. Finding so many more compared to how it was before proves that the word about Kirakee's help is getting around, and they are turning up safely in the right place.

But she does wonder who it was that was sending the wolves to the witch when they were seeking her help?

Tick Tock sits staring in silence at Kirakee.

Kirakee stares back at Tick Tock, and it occurs to her that the snow has fallen. She wonders whether Tarkin and Sheena need help.

'I've just thought of something I need to do. I think it's about time I make a trip to help Stark look after Tarkin and Sheena throughout the snow season. I'll head off in a few days,' she smiles.

She goes around to each of her guests, planning for each of them to take on a responsible role while she is absent. Each one will be able to contribute to the health and safety of the pack.

Now that she knows the strengths of each of the members, she assigns suitable roles to each and everyone. She assigns more responsibility to the strongest member of the pack.

'Could you please supervise every day each member's role while I'm away?'

'Sure, thing Kirakee. How long will you be away for?'

'I'll return when the snow melts,' she smiles.

'Hello, mother.'

Kirakee quickly turns around. 'Hi, Omega Sunset. This is a surprise. What are you doing here? Is everything alright?'

'Sorry, mother, for turning up without you knowing, but I didn't know what else to do,' she sadly says.

Kirakee walks over to Omega Sunset and snuggles closely to her. 'Come inside. You can tell me what is wrong.'

They walk into the deepest and darkest area of the den and sit down.

'What has happened, Omega Sunset?'

'I had an argument with father because he doesn't like one of my friends. I sneaked outside, but he found out who I was with. He doesn't like any of my friends.'

'I'm sorry to hear that. What is it about your friend that your father doesn't like?'

'He doesn't like him because he comes from a different territory. It's not fair because he has been my best friend and always looks after me.'

'Hmm... that's a difficult one. I think you need to talk it over with your father. He will be upset with you for coming here without him knowing where you are; he will be worried about your safety too. You really need to go home very soon.'

Omega Sunset looks stressed. 'Please don't make me go home right now. Can I stay here with you?'

'I don't mind if you stay here, little one, but staying here will most likely upset him even more. It would be best that you let him know where you are.' Kirakee takes a deep breath. 'Come, we will go and see him together.'

Omega Sunset expresses how she feels as they walk home to Mud's place. 'Mother, I want to live with you too,' she sobs.

'I'd love for you to live with me too, but I don't think you could stay where I am right now. I couldn't have you stay there with all the other members of the pack.'

'Could you find another place to live, mother?'

'Well, if you are sure that's what you want, I guess I could find or make a home nearby to the big den. It would be a steppingstone for us until we could find something bigger or better.'

'Oh, really, mother? That would be great. I've really missed you.'

Kirakee stops walking and gently snuggles her head closely to Omega Sunset. 'I've missed you too, little one, but you will need to let your father know what you are doing.'

As they approach Mud's den, Mud runs outside. He is clearly upset.

'Where have you been? I've been looking for you everywhere,' he growls.

Omega Sunset is nervous; she trembles. 'I went to see mother and have come back to ask if I can stay at her place tonight?'

'No, you can't,' he growls.

Kirakee snuggles closely to her daughter and whispers in her ear. 'Talk to him tomorrow when he calms down.'

'Okay, mother. Will you find another place for us to live? I want to come and stay tomorrow,' she whispers.

'I will. I'll get on to looking for something when I get back home,' Kirakee smiles.

Back at home, she begins looking for another new den nearby.

Under a fallen tree, supported by large rocks on a hillside, she digs out a den from an opening in the rocks. Her effort to create a suitable den causes her to work into the late hours of the night. The snow is thick; she must make sure the new den is secure from the snowfall, so it does not bury the entrance.

'I think this will be good for now,' she whispers to herself.

As she feels a sense of calm after a surge of excitement, later the next day, she heads back over to Mud's den to collect her daughter.

'Hello, little one. Are you ready to go? Is everything okay?'

'Yes, mother. Father is in a better mood today like you said he would be.'

'That's good to know. How was he when you told him about you coming to live with me some of the time?'

'He didn't say very much,' she sheepishly says.

'You sure he is okay with you coming to live with me some of the time?' Kirakee asks.

'Yes, mother. It will be fine. Don't worry.'

Back at their new den, Omega Sunset and Kirakee work together to tidy up their den. Omega Sunset is excited. She asks Kirakee often whether there is anything she can do to help with chores, wanting to feel like she is contributing.

They laugh and play around in the snow.

After a few days, Kirakee must take Omega Sunset home. They are beginning to build a bond.

Spending time with any of her pups now is another responsibility she had not planned for, and she realizes she cannot leave and help Stark to take care of Tarkin and Sheena. She feels saddened that she must let them down.

She tells Tick Tock to inform Stark about her reason for not being with them. She then asks Tick Tock to provide her with an ongoing report about their wellbeing.

Upon one of her new pack members hearing of Kirakee asking Tick Tock to check on her friends, he comes over to her.

'Who are these friends you speak of, Kirakee?'

'They are very loyal friends. They helped me through a difficult time, and every snow season, I work to help them survive the weather,' she smiles.

'That's good of you, Kirakee, but why would they need your help? It's a tough time for all of us. Are they old?'

'No, they're not old. Just very different than the rest of us,' she smiles.

Kirakee does not want to reveal too much information about Tarkin and Sheena for two reasons. They will not believe her, and she is keeping Tarkin and Sheena's location private for their own safety.

She walks into her cave, where most of her new pack are huddled up, keeping themselves out from the cold. 'Hey guys, could you all pitch in to clean out the den? It's getting a bit grubby in here and becoming a health hazard.'

Everyone gets to their feet and begins digging around in the cave. Outside, a snowstorm has begun to blow more snow into the entrance, and considering her own small den, she heads back to her own and clears the snow from it blocking the entrance.

Feeling a little tired, she lays down and falls asleep. She dreams of her friends, Stark, Tarkin and Sheena.

A Rescue

Chapter 20

The next morning, she wakes to hearing her name being called. Overnight the snow has covered the entrance of the den once again, so she must frantically dig out the snow first before she can go outside and see who is calling for her.

She finally breaks the snow and the daylight streams into her eyes. She blinks a few times to clear her vision and then sticks her head outside.

'Kirakee, Kirakee, where are you?' Tick Tock shouts.

Tick Tock is standing on a tree branch near the entrance of her guest den.

'I'm here, Tick Tock,' she says as she runs towards him.

Tick Tock looks stressed, and he is panting. 'Kirakee, there is trouble.

You need to come with me. Sheena has been captured by humans.'

'Gasp!'

'I don't think she is coming back either,' says Tick Tock.

'Do you know where they have taken her, my friend?'

'Yes, they have her in a large cage. The cage is covered, but I could hear her calling out. She needs our help, Kirakee.'

'Okay, okay. Let me think for a minute about what to do?'

Tick Tock flutters down to another branch closer to Kirakee. 'Stark is waiting for us with Tarkin,' he whispers.

'Where are they waiting, Tick Tock?'

'At Tarkin and Sheena's cave. I told them I would return with you?'

'Of course, but I don't know what any of us can do, especially dealing with man is dangerous, and we are no match for them alone,' she says sadly.

Upon hearing Tick Tock and Kirakee's conversation, a guest member comes out of the cave. 'I couldn't help hearing of your troubles. Sounds like you will need some more help. I would like to help you and your friends.'

Kirakee smiles. 'Thank you, but I really will need you to stay here and take care of the other pack members while I'm away.'

'No, you won't need to worry about that, Kirakee,' she hears another voice coming out from within the cave. 'I want to help too.'

The remaining pack members come out of the cave. There is murmuring and chattering within the pack. She can hear all of them saying, 'Me too.'

She stares at them in silence for a moment, wondering if she should allow them to be involved. It would mean revealing Tarkin's and Sheena's existence. But she knows she can't risk losing the chance to save Sheena.

'Okay, okay, thank you, but I need you to know. By helping us to save my friend, you would also be risking your own life as well. We are dealing with humans. You can tell me now if you are having second thoughts about helping. I will respect your decision—whichever one you choose.'

The pack all murmur and chatter amongst themselves.

'No, we have decided; we are all coming too.'

Kirakee takes a deep breath. 'Okay, great! Let's go!'

She begins running as she follows Tick Tock flying in front of her while the rest of the pack pursue.

The snow is deep, and the depth of snow is tiring the whole pack as they try to navigate through the woods, hilltops, and open terrain.

'Kirakee, we will need to stop at the cave to collect Stark,' Tick Tock says.

Kirakee is panting while she is running and struggles to speak. 'Do you think that will be a good thing to do since we have everyone else with us?'

Tick Tock slows down and flutters over Kirakee. 'It will be okay. They can stay down at the base of the hill and guard the surroundings while we collect Stark.'

One of the closet members can clearly hear what Tick Tock and Kirakee are talking about. 'Who is Stark?' he asks.

Kirakee quickly looks back. 'He is a friend. You will see.'

As they approach the base of the hilltop, Kirakee stops and turns to face the pack.

'Please, stay here and keep guard. Tick Tock and I will be back soon.'

In the cave, she finds Stark and Tarkin huddled up, trying to keep warm.

'Hey, it's me,' she says with a smile.

Stark and Tarkin stand up quickly on their feet.

Stark wags his tail. 'We are so glad to see you.'

'I'm glad to see you are safe. I came as quickly as I could. So, are you ready for us to get Sheena back?' she pants.

'I sure am, but this is not going to be an easy rescue. How are we ever going to be able to rescue her with just me, you and Stark?' Tarkin sadly says.

Kirakee moves close to Tarkin and looks him straight in the eyes. 'We will be able to do it, my friend. I brought with me some help. Have faith, we have this covered.'

'Help. Who is helping?' Stark asks with a curious expression.

Kirakee smiles. 'Look down at the base of the hill. You will see.'

Stark moves out to the opening of the cave and looks down the hill. 'Gasp! Who are they?' he asks.

'They are from a few different territories. They are the ones who have been abandoned, so I found them, and now they have become my pack.'

Stark looks back over his shoulder to Kirakee. He stares at her for a moment in silence. 'Well, what are we waiting for?' he chuckles.

Tarkin moves to the entrance so he can have a look too, but Kirakee has different thoughts.

'No, Tarkin, you shouldn't let everyone else see you. It would be much safer if we could keep you a secret for the sake of your safety.'

Tarkin stops upon hearing her warning. 'Okay, Kirakee, you are so right. I trust what you are saying.'

'It's for the best, Tarkin. By the way, how did Sheena get into all this mess? How did she get captured?'

Tarkin shakes his head. 'You know Sheena. She still hasn't learned from experience.' Tarkin sighs. 'Just before the snow fell, she heard human voices outside. She just couldn't help herself, she had to look outside, and by doing that, she was seen by the humans. Instead of running back into the cave to hide, she ran in the opposite direction. Maybe she was trying to lure them away from our home?

'When she didn't come back by sundown, I went looking for her. I found her in a trapper's net, dangling from a tree. I tried to bring the net down but just couldn't make it move. I tried until the next sunrise, and that's when I had to stop because I could hear the voices of men once again.

'I ran back up to our cave, and from there, I watched the humans bring Sheena down in the net and lock her in a large cage. There was nothing I could do to stop them,' he sadly says.

Kirakee exhales. 'You did your best, Tarkin. Don't worry, we will do our best to try and get her back, but you must stay here while we look for her. No one else needs to know you are here. Okay?'

Tarkin nods in agreement.

As Stark, Kirakee, and Tick Tock reach the base of the hill, Kirakee introduces Stark to every other member of the pack.

Stark and Kirakee plan how they will approach the rescue. Stark orders the biggest pack members to coordinate the pack's moves as they approach the humans.

'I need you to seek out the slowest of the pack and put them towards the front of the pack, so Kirakee, Tick Tock, and I can make sure they are keeping up with us.'

Kirakee gives instructions on how they will approach the humans camp area.

'When we arrive, no one is to randomly run into the camp. We don't want to stir up a panic. But we will encircle the surroundings, and when it looks peaceful, we enter the camp area together while Stark goes in to free our imprisoned friend. Is everyone clear on that?'

The pack look around amongst themselves. There is a loud murmuring and chatting amongst them as they make sure everyone agrees.

Kirakee takes a deep breath. 'Okay, and Tick Tock, once we are close by to the camp area, we will need you to fly ahead of us to make sure they are still there and then report back to us before we head in.'

Tick Tock nods in agreement.

They have been traveling for a day and slowly gaining ground on the camp area.

As they all draw closer, the smell of smoke dominates what was once crisp, clear air.

'I think we are close to where they are, Tick Tock. You will need to go ahead and check.'

Tick Tock flies off, and within a few minutes, he arrives back.

'They are just over the hill ahead of us. I couldn't hear Sheena, though, but there is a cage within their sight, and it's covered.'

Kirakee is beginning to feel a little nervous; she takes a deep breath and exhales sharply.

'Thanks, Tick Tock. You hear that, everyone? Remember the plan. Please follow the instructions.'

They encircle the camp area. There is a tent with a soft light emitting from within. Nearby is a smoldering campfire, and next to both is a large snow sled with Sheena's cage sitting on top of the sled. The cage is loosely tied down by a large set of ropes.

Kirakee turns and faces the pack. 'Okay, guys. Stay on this side, right here on the outskirts, and Stark and I will quietly check out the cage to see if our friend is still in there.'

Stark and Kirakee walk quietly over to the cage and sniff around the cage until Stark finds an opening in the cover.

'She is here,' Stark whispers as he has vision of Sheena.

Kirakee puts her head into the opening of the cover. 'Sheena, wake up,' she whispers.

Sheena slowly stirs. 'Hmm, did someone call my name,' she says.

'Hush,' Kirakee whispers.

Sheena quickly jumps to her feet. 'Kirakee, Stark. So good to see you guys. Please get me out of here,' she roars.

'We are going to try, but you have to stay quiet,' Kirakee whispers.

Behind them, they hear a sudden rustle. It is one of the men who has now come out of the tent to investigate the noise.

Kirakee and Stark turn around. Both gasp with shock.

The man is holding his hands up above his head, taking a step back. 'Woe, fellas,' he says.

The other man sticks his head out of the tent upon hearing his companion. He steps outside and is startled to see they have new company. He, too, puts his hands up above his head alongside his friend.

'Take it easy, guys. Take it easy,' he says as he steps back.

The whole pack are in a half-circle in their camp. They slowly advance on the men, growling and snarling.

Kirakee jumps forward in front of the pack. She snarls. 'Let them go. They don't have guns.' She snaps at the pack

One of the pack members growls. 'They will come back and cause us harm.'

The pack continue to advance closer to the humans, causing the men to step back further towards the thickness of the forest.

Kirakee is angered, the pack are not following instructions. 'Stop! I told you. Let them go now,' she yells.

The whole pack freeze as they stare at Kirakee and the men. The men turn around and speedily run off into the forest.

'See, I told you. They don't have any guns. They are just as scared as we are, and best to let them go.'

Stark walks over to Kirakee. He looks puzzled. 'Well, we have what we came here for, but I can't see how we can free her.'

'Don't worry, Stark. We will work that out later. Right now, we just need to get out of here even with her still stuck in there, so what we will have to do is drag everything through the snow until we get her home.'

'Oh, that isn't going to be easy, Kirakee,' Stark says with a frown.

'Maybe not, Stark, but we can only try with all of us working together by pulling it with those ropes.'

'Okay, you're right. I'll instruct everyone on how to do it.'

Stark shows the pack what they need to do. All of them grab hold of the ropes and begin pulling the sled.

'You are all doing a great job. Just a little more to go, and once we are on top of that hill, it's easy-going from there on,' Stark encourages.

177

Pulling the sled uphill is hard. The pack pull and pull with great strength, but as they make it to the highest point of the hill, no one expects what the pull of gravity will do.

On the other side of the hill, the slope is steeper, and the snowy hillside is no challenge for them. Suddenly they lose grip of the ropes as the sled begins to slide down the hill all by itself.

The pack begin running after it, but its speed is too fast for them to keep up.

Just as they are halfway down the hill with the sled near the bottom, the sled tumbles over and begins rolling until it smashes into the base of the slope.

Out comes tumbling Sheena from the broken cage. She lets out a great roar as she lands flat in the open snow.

Most of the pack stop running halfway down the hill, frozen in

their step. Gasps come from the pack. The gasps turn into yelps.

'That's one messed up looking wolf,' says one of the pack members.

Most of the pack members turn around and run off in different directions.

'Come back here, you guys,' Kirakee yells out.

Stark burst into laughter. 'Ha, ha, they didn't expect our friend to look like that.'

Kirakee looks at Stark and giggles. 'Well, that's the end of that. isn't it?'

'Yep! Let them go. They'll find their way home,' Stark chuckles.

Sheena looks bewildered. 'What's wrong with them,' she asks.

Kirakee walks over to Sheena. 'Don't worry about it, Sheena. They just thought we were rescuing another wolf. They didn't expect to see you,' she giggles.

Stark walks over to Sheena and Kirakee. 'Well, my friends, I never thought we could do it, but we did, and now everyone is safe. We all need to quickly return to our homes.'

Kirakee looks at Sheena. 'Yes, home for sure, but I'm thinking you guys will be needing a new home after this. I don't feel you are going to be safe living where you are now since the humans have already been in that area.'

Stark and Sheena agree. Now they will have to break the news to Tarkin.

When Sheena arrives back at her home, Tarkin is so happy to see her. He jumps all over her.

'I was beginning to think I'd never see you again,' Tarkin says.

They all sit down together and discuss their options for relocating Sheena and Tarkin.

'I think it would be best if you both come and live in my territory,' says Kirakee.

Tarkin is concerned. 'Is it going to be any safer than here, though,' asks Tarkin.

Kirakee smiles. 'I think so, Tarkin. If Sheena doesn't reveal herself to any humans ever again,' she chuckles.

Sheena nods in agreement. 'Don't worry about that ever happening again. I've learned my lesson for good.'

Kirakee nods. 'Yes, so I guess we are set then. I think we better get moving soon before nightfall.'

They all set off towards Kirakee's territory with Tick Tock flying above while he looks out for any danger as they travel back through the snowy terrains.

Kirakee looks at Sheena and Tarkin. 'I think I know of a good place for you to stay. It's not very far away from where I am living, but it's far enough away, so you won't be bothered by any of the other wolves.'

'Will you and Stark be seeing us very much while we live in this new place you mention?' Tarkin asks.

'Yes, for sure. Stark and I will still take care of you through the snow season, and you are very welcome to join my guest pack at any time, too, Stark. That's if you'd like too?' Kirakee asks.

Stark looks surprised. 'Are you sure I'd be welcome by your guests, though, Kirakee?'

'Oh yes, you will find they are very accepting. They've been through some very tough times, and they are not ones to judge who you are or where you have come from.'

They arrive at the new den for Tarkin and Sheena, only to discover it's very small.

'I know it is very small, but it would be better for warmth through the snow season. I think you will find this is going to be very comfortable for both of you,' Kirakee smiles.

Stark looks at Kirakee. 'Well, I can't see myself being able to stay there very much. It isn't big enough for three of us.'

'That's not going to be a problem, Stark. Like I said, you can always stay where I am at any time. At least you and I won't be too far away from Tarkin and Sheena.'

For the next day, Stark and Kirakee go out scavenging for food for Sheena and Tarkin. Stark decides to stay with his big cat friends for the first few days until they are settled in.

As Kirakee walks back to her home, she thinks about what kind of things are going to be said about what happened with the rescue of Sheena. *'What am I going to say to explain who Sheena is? I'll have to ask them not to tell any other wolf packs for the sake of their safety.'*

As Kirakee walks back into her territory, her guests come out of their cave one by one. She can hear whispers.

'Has she come back alone?' whispers one of her pack members.

They all just stand still and stare at her as she walks over. Then there is silence.

Kirakee stares back at them for a moment.

'Okay, okay, guys. It's me. I'm not a ghost or something. You don't need to look so shocked,' she giggles.

'Ha, good to see you have made it back here safely,' says one of the pack members.

Kirakee smiles. 'There was never a problem, guys. Of course, I was always going to make it back safely. So, if any of you have any questions, it would be a good time to ask me now?'

The pack look around at each other with a curious look on their faces as if to ask if anyone is going to speak.

One of them steps forward. 'I think we are all lost for words. Could you please fill us in on what we all need to know?'

Kirakee exhales. 'Well, could I ask all of you to do us all a favour by not revealing every single detail of what you saw at our rescue?'

They all look around amongst themselves and mumble. After a brief consultation with each other, they reassemble about-face in front of Kirakee.

One of the members steps forward. 'Yes, of course, we agree. Our lips are sealed.'

'Great. Thank you. I will tell you more later, but right now, the less you know, the better it will be for all of us, and by the way, we have got a lot of work to do right now, so let's focus on surviving the next snowstorm. And since I'll be busy spending more time with my daughter, I ask our biggest pack members to please supervise the pack while I'm away at times?' she says.

They all nod in agreement.

Kirakee turns around and begins to walk away. She looks back over her shoulder. 'I'll be back later. I'm off to collect my daughter Omega Sunset.'

As she walks, she is feeling a sense of pride because she has accomplished so much. Her pack have shown their strengths, she is now making a mother-daughter relationship, and she is now able to be with Stark, Tarkin, and Sheena once again.

Defamed

Chapter 21

'Mother, mother,' Omega Sunset calls out as she excitedly runs over to Kirakee.

'Hey, little one. I'm so glad to see you,' Kirakee snuggles closely with her daughter.

'I've missed you, mother.'

'I've missed you too. So, are you ready to come back over home?'

Omega Sunset looks up to Kirakee. She has a look of concern on her face. 'Umm, I will have to ask father first.'

'You must ask your father? Doesn't he know you are coming to my place today?' Kirakee is surprised.

Omega Sunset puts her head down. 'No, he doesn't know yet,' she sadly says.

'Okay, that's not a big problem. I'll come with you while you ask him. He needs to know, doesn't he?'

Omega Sunset goes inside Mud's den while Kirakee waits outside. She can hear some growling coming from inside the den. A few minutes later, Mud comes out. He looks angry.

'I don't want my daughter staying at your place. It is not a suitable place for a young wolf to be,' he snaps.

Kirakee looks confused. 'I don't know what you are worried about, Mud. The new den might not be far from my pack's cave, but it isn't in the thick of the pack. I've made sure we have a comfortable place to live.'

Mud growls. 'A comfortable place to live. She's not living with you. She can stay for a visit, but that's it,' he snaps.

'I don't know what you are talking about, Mud. Omega Sunset told me she had told you she is going to be living with me too, and you didn't say anything to disagree.'

Mud jumps forward at Kirakee. 'She never told me she was going to be living with you at all. I knew nothing about it,' he growls.

Their daughter steps outside of the den. 'I'm sorry, mother. I never got the chance to tell father,' she nervously says.

Mud turns around and snaps. 'Go inside!'

'Don't take it out on her, Mud. She just didn't get the chance to tell you. Maybe she was worried that you wouldn't let her be with me. She does have a right to be with me, too, you know. She is coming with me now. Omega Sunset, please come outside. We are going,' Kirakee calls out.

Her daughter emerges from the den.

Kirakee walks over to her. 'Come on, little one. We are going.'

Kirakee worries about what Mud says, she knows how he can cause her more problems, but she feels she must do what she can for Omega Sunset.

185

Omega Sunset looks extremely stressed. 'I want to be with you, too, mother, but I don't want to be making father angry. It makes me feel bad.'

Kirakee stops walking and looks down at her. 'You aren't doing anything wrong. Your father shouldn't be making you feel so bad.'

'He was angry that I stayed at your place the other day. Father and Pit left me out of doing things with them. Instead, Lunar, Night, Pit, her daughter, and father shared things but didn't offer me any. I was made to feel like I have done something wrong.'

Kirakee's heart sinks. She feels saddened knowing that Omega Sunset has been suffering. 'Oh, I'm so sorry. They shouldn't be doing things like that to you. They are just trying to make you feel like you have done something wrong because they don't want you spending time with me.'

Over the next few weeks, Kirakee juggles her time with Stark, Tarkin, Sheena, and her pack while she makes time with her youngest daughter every few days.

Now her eldest daughter Lunar has begun to visit occasionally, but Mud's disapproval of everything and the strain Omega Sunset is feeling is beginning to take a toll on her daughter. She is beginning to rebel more than ever before.

The mother-daughter pair argue.

The situation escalates, and the argument becomes more aggressive. Omega Sunset says a great deal more hurtful things to Kirakee and deliberately criticizes Kirakee's good intentions.

Upon disciplining Omega Sunset by taking away privileges, she immediately returns to Mud's den out of defiance.

A few hours later, Mud arrives at Kirakee's den. He is angry. 'What kind of mother are you to upset your daughter like that?'

Kirakee snaps. 'You obviously don't know all the facts.'

Mud jumps forward, snapping. 'You don't even know how to be a proper mother. You originally dumped your pups on to me, and I'm still taking care of their feelings and picking up all the pieces.'

Feeling anxious about Mud's intentions to rid her out of her pups' lives again, she plans to see Night since she has not seen him for a while. But upon searching for him, she sees Night traveling through the woods with Morana.

When Morana departs from Kirakee's son, she decides it is a good time to approach him. Their greeting goes well, but upon Night hearing of Kirakee's woes with his father, he becomes defensive and criticizes Kirakee. Mud has already been putting ideas in Night's head about how he views Kirakee's current position with Omega Sunset.

Kirakee attempts to provide Night with the real facts, but he has already made his mind up and criticizes Kirakee about her position in the territory and family compared to Morana.

'Well, mother, Morana isn't the way you say she is. In fact, she is my best friend, and she has done more for me in recent times than you have done,' he sarcastically says.

Kirakee's heart drops a beat. She can feel her heartbreaking. 'How could you say that to me, Night. It's not all my fault I haven't been able to do much for you for a while. Remember when I was going through a tough time when your father wasn't of any help. I wanted to make things right with you, but you turned your back on me. I can't believe you would call your aunt your best friend just like that after all that has happened,' she sobs.

'Oh, so now you are trying to make me feel guilty. Is that it, mother? I'll just forget we had this conversation because you are being a whimpering Nancy,' he snaps.

Kirakee looks up at him; she is shocked. Now she must deal with him having an opinion of her.

'Wow, Night, that's just so rude, and do you know what? You are just sounding like your father, and if you don't snap out of it, you are going to end up being like him.'

As she begins to walk off, Night calls out.

'Well, that's not such a bad thing. At least he is happy,' he smugly says.

Kirakee stops and looks back. 'Okay, if you are going to be like that towards me, and while you are with Morana, then I guess I shouldn't expect you to be having any interest in what I'm doing.'

'Okay, mother. No problem,' he smugly says.

While walking away, she shakes her head as she tries to comprehend what has just happened. She just cannot get over how her own pups have turned on her, and they just can't see the wrongdoings of Morana or Mud.

As Night disappears further into the thickness of the forest, a rustling sound is above her. She looks up.

'Hi, Tick Tock. I guess I don't need to tell you about what just happened. You probably already know again?'

'Yes!' Tick Tock flutters and nods his head.

Talk is spreading around throughout the territories, questioning Kirakee's parenting style. Rumors are flourishing.

Upon venturing into the forest, Kirakee is confronted by a pack of the territory wolves. They criticize Kirakee about what kind of mother they think she is based on the rumors they have heard.

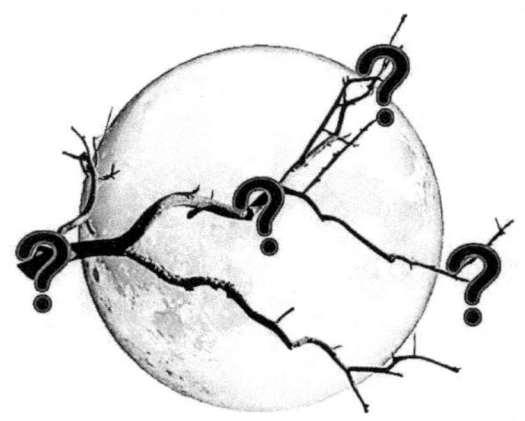

All Truths
Revealed in Good Time

Chapter
22

Feeling the need to remove herself from the territory to give herself a break, she receives news: Mist has now joined Alfa Noon's pack.

The very next day, she heads off to their territory.

She can see Mist ahead of her. 'Mist, Mist, it's me, Kirakee,' she yells out.

Mist stops walking and turns around.

'Hello Kirakee, what are you doing here?' he wags his tail.

Kirakee walks up to him. 'Good to see you again, Mist. I was coming to see you and catch up with our son.'

Mist looks puzzled. 'Why would you be coming to see me?'

Kirakee takes a deep breath and exhales. 'I would like to clear the air with you about things that happened many seasons ago. I have questions and would like to make sure you know about some facts, so you will understand I didn't have anything to do with terrible things that happened to you back then.' She inhales.

Mist moves over to Kirakee. They sit down together.

'I would like you to know, Mist, that I was never involved with Morana and her friends bullying you. I had nothing to do with it.'

Mist frowns. 'What bullying are you talking about?'

'Morana told me how she and her friends teased you when you were with your friends. They walked behind you and were making fun of you because you weren't involved in Alfa Noon's life.'

Mist looks angry. 'No! Morana never bullied me. Her friends did, though.'

'Yes, she did, Mist; she told me she did.'

'No, that's not right, Kirakee. Morana told me she wasn't the one who bullied me. She said her friends were doing all the talking, and she just happened to be there.'

'Oh, so you've talked to Morana about this then. Well, she is lying. She did bully you because she came home bragging about it, telling me everything she said, like as if she was feeling proud of herself.'

Mist hangs his head down. He looks sad. 'Well, I don't believe that. She wouldn't do that to me. I believed her.'

Kirakee is feeling upset. 'Why are you sticking up for her, Mist? She is a troublemaker, and when she did, I was very hurt too. I didn't want you hurt, and it also hurt me to think you would blame me for that happening to you. I'd never encourage or do a thing like that.'

Mist shakes his head. 'Well, I don't know. I believed her.'

191

'She can't be trusted, Mist. She has caused me so much trouble, and I want to ask you another thing. I never was able to ask Morana what she said to you that day you walked out on me when I told you I was pregnant.

You started to talk to me about what we should do, and then she interrupted. You privately spoke to her about something. I've always had a feeling she said something to make you leave. What did you and her talk about?'

'She told me you didn't want to be with me, and you didn't want to join my territory pack.'

Kirakee is shocked. She gasps. 'Well, she lied, Mist. I never said anything like that.'

Mist stares at Kirakee in silence for a moment. 'Morana said you had talked to her about it, and you said you didn't want anything to do with it all, and you know me with how it was with my territory pack members. I could only support you having Alfa Noon if you were accepted into my pack, and to do that, you had to want to be a part of my pack and territory.'

Kirakee is feeling stunned at this moment. She knew Morana had interfered and caused trouble in other things before and since, but she just cannot get over why Morana would be so cruel to stop Mist from being in her and Alfa Noon's life.

'I'm sorry, Mist, but she lied, and because she was of no help, you missed out on being in Alfa Noon's life for so long.'

'But I didn't miss out entirely,' Mist frowns. 'She helped me and Alfa Noon to see each other again and often, right up to a few seasons ago.'

Kirakee's heart is racing. She is learning now just how much she has been fooled by Morana. 'What? She helped you up until a few seasons ago. She has lied to me and you. Many times, I looked for you so you and Alfa Noon could be together. I went to see an old friend of ours, and he told me he would pass on any

192

information to Morana for her to let me know. Also, she lied to me about her intentions. She never told me you and she had spoken.'

'Oh well, it doesn't matter now. It is in the past,' Mist says.

'It isn't quite in the past though, Mist, because this proves what she has done is what she can do, and she is still doing it. She has manipulated the outcome of our relationships. She must stop!'

'Well, I don't know what to think now. I still have my own opinion of things,' Mist says.

Kirakee stares at Mist for a moment, trying to figure out what Mist does not quite understand clearly for him to have his own opinion of things.

'You know the truth now, Mist. You shouldn't be making excuses for Morana. She hasn't changed.'

Kirakee is feeling rather stressed and angered. She needs to comprehend all she has learned.

'I'm going now, Mist. I'll see Alfa Noon on my way home. Take care of yourself,' she says as she walks away.

Angered by the news, she heads back towards her territory with the stride of a soldier heading into battle.

As she walks, she can hear the rustling of Tick Tock's wings above her. She knows he is there.

'You know, don't you?' she says.

'Yeah!' says Tick Tock.

Kirakee doesn't look up at Tick Tock; she is focused on looking ahead.

'I've got to stop her. Morana has never acted like a sister. She has been a nightmare,' she angrily says.

Tick Tock is silent for a moment. 'I understand, Kirakee, but you really need to think this through. If you confront her over this, she probably will just discredit you again.'

Kirakee stops and looks up at Tick Tock. 'I've been wondering the same thing.'

Tick Tock flutters closer to Kirakee and whispers, 'I think it is time you plan.'

Kirakee chuckles. 'True that. Anyone would think you are my wolf shadow in owls' feathers.'

'Well, I'm quite happy to be more than just your shadow Kirakee,' he smiles.

Kirakee begins walking again and thinks about what she should do. *I need to start with the Legends and talk to them about Morana. They will be able to tell me what I should do.*

'You know what, Tick Tock? I'm going to get this off my chest and go straight to the Legends pack and tell them everything. Let them be my judge and jury.'

She walks straight toward the Legends pack territory. As she approaches, she howls to the pack. Some of the pack are standing outside their den, and upon hearing her howl, the remaining pack members come outside to investigate.

'What is it, Kirakee?'

Kirakee stands before the gathered pack and requests their help. She explains everything to them about all her problems. She tells them all about Morana. The things she has done with interfering in her relationships , the trouble -making , the lies, the theft, the insults, and the assault.

'Well, Kirakee, you certainly have a lot of problems going on in your life, and I totally agree with you coming to us to find answers. My best advice would be to keep away from Morana and her toxic ways.'

Kirakee stares in silence for a moment at the wise old wolf. 'Well, yes, I've tried that, though, but she always finds a way to still interfere in my life. It's like she follows me everywhere.'

One by one, each member speaks their own judgment and their opinion.

'I think you should distance yourself from your pups, and when they need you, let them come to you. But when they do, state your ground and your rules. They need to learn to respect you.'

Kirakee smiles. 'Yes, I've tried that.'

Another member speaks. 'I think you were right trying to stop Morana from seeing your pups, and she should have stayed away from your family. I agree; she is a troublemaker.'

Kirakee nods. 'Yes.'

Another member speaks. 'I think you have every reason to be angry and upset with Mud as well for not cooperating with you, especially since he said, 'Morana is a troublemaker.' You have every right to be annoyed with him for him siding with Morana.'

Kirakee nods. 'Yes, so true.'

Another member speaks. 'Well, I think you should have just belted her up.'

All the Legends pack and Kirakee look straight at him with surprise and gasp.

'Well, I don't think that would exactly resolve everything for Kirakee,' one of the members says with a frown.

Kirakee stands up. 'Okay, so what should I do about Morana? She shouldn't be able to believe she can get away with everything still.'

The oldest of the wolves stands up and walks over to Kirakee. 'Just leave it with us, Kirakee. We are going to tell whoever needs to know, so we can warn others about Morana, that's if we have any reports of her defaming, you again.'

Kirakee feels a little more relieved that the Legends pack are going to help and happy they empathize with her side of things.

'She has a way of getting at me in so many ways. I'm so sick of her calling me names like Witches poo, etc.,' she says with her head hanging down in shame.

'Witches poo? Good grief, why would she call you that?' asks one of the members.

Kirakee explains to the pack how Morana began calling her that name after a witch had moved into the woods near Morakee. She tells them how she recently found out about how this witch had begun calling herself Kirakee as well. She explains how she and Tuck had gone to see the witch after they found out the wolves were being sent to the witch when they had been looking for her, and she warned the witch that if she didn't stop using her name and taking the spirit of the wolves, then she would return with the Legend pack to rid her of the forest.

'She actually sounded quite nervous, and even more so when I told her I would return with all of you,' she says with a chuckle.

Gasps come from the members. 'This is serious, Kirakee. You should have told us sooner.'

'Umm, sorry. I thought I could take care of it at the time and would let you know if the witch continued, but I believe she has stopped taking the spirit of the wolves after I warned her because more downtrodden wolves have been coming to me since they are not being harmed.'

Another old wise wolf stands up. 'I remember one of our old wise wolves speaking to me about a spirit Witch living in the woods near Morakee.'

Kirakee's eyes widen. 'So, what did he tell you?' she asks.

'He never got around to telling me everything about the witch. We were interrupted, and he never got to finish what he was

196

wanting to tell me.'

Kirakee wants to know more. 'Where is he now? We should ask him to tell us more,' she says with a concerned frown.

The wise wolf looks at Kirakee and stares in silence for a moment. 'I'm afraid that is not possible, Kirakee, because the very next day, he was taken from us. Shot dead by humans,' he sadly says.

Kirakee gasps.

'I know, it was tragic, and it happened when he was heading over to the spirit witch's territory.'

Kirakee's mouth hangs open in shock. She stares for a moment. 'So why was he going over to see the witch?'

'Well, I'm not entirely sure of all the details, but I do remember something else.'

He pauses, takes a deep breath, looks straight at Kirakee, and then exhales.

'I do remember him telling me something else, which was a few weeks before his death. He said he had spoken to your aunt, and it had something to do with the daughters of Morakee, but he didn't explain anything else to me.

Shortly after, he was going to see the spirit witch in the forest because he had been informed, she was stirring up trouble for one of the daughters of Morakee. He was handling the situation as if it was an urgent matter.'

'Morakee's daughters? Who was he talking about? Doesn't anyone else know?' Kirakee asks.

'I have asked the same questions, Kirakee, but it's becoming clear, we should start asking your aunt questions, but I was of the impression that someone else had spoken to her not so long after.'

Kirakee shakes her head to try and clear her thoughts and then stares for a moment. 'You know, I think whatever you were meant to be told has been a problem that has been going on for an awfully long time. Maybe not as a big of a problem back in the early days, but somehow the problem escalated into something bigger in more recent days,' she says with a frown.

'You're right, Kirakee. I'm stunned that we haven't known more about what has been happening a lot sooner,' says a member.

There are gasps amongst the Legends pack, then complete silence. Kirakee looks up and is stunned to see all the members just staring at her with questionable looks on their faces.

She gasps. 'What is it, what's happening?' she frowns.

One of the Legends members stands up and slowly walks towards Kirakee. He has fixed eye contact with her. 'Maybe it's you, Kirakee? It makes sense. You are one of the daughters of Morakee. You've had trouble. The witch has used your name to deceive the wolves of the forest and discredit you. Maybe, you are the one who the witch has been targeting.'

Kirakee is lost for words. She stands to her feet and looks around at the Legends pack member while they still have their eyes fixed on her.

She shakes her head, then takes a deep breath. 'So, what else can I say. Why me? If that's even correct, but I just don't understand. I see the witch has been wreaking havoc on the wolves in the forest, but my biggest threat has been my sister, Morana.'

'I understand, Kirakee. I think it's about time we all spend more time paying attention to this to find more answers, but in the meantime, please let us handle Morana for you.'

Kirakee trusts the Legends pack with her life for them to do as they say, so she leaves the matter with them. She bids the Legend pack farewell and heads back to her territory.

Pet Talk

Chapter 23

Feeling frustrated that she can't vent her anger to Morana based on the Legend wolf pack planning to take care of any issues that might arise with Morana, she spends the following days going about her daily duties, but her thoughts are consumed with what is suspected about the forest witch.

A few days later, she receives news from the Legends pack. 'Mud's new partner has lost the plot and run off with one of the young wolf members.'

Immediately after, Omega Sunset turns to Kirakee for support because she is having issues with her own sister, Lunar.

After they had grown old enough, the two moved into a den of their own. Her daughters' relationship has become divided, and they are beginning to remind Kirakee of everything she has endured with Morana.

Kirakee advises Omega Sunset to never allow what she has seen of herself, and her aunt Morana's situation ever be an example to think that it is okay because it is not, and it is not normal.

Kirakee offers Omega Sunset for her to talk to Lunar, but Omega Sunset expresses her concerns.

'No, mother. Don't say anything to her. It will only make things worse. She will think that you are saying something to her would be like an attack on her.'

It has become obvious that Omega Sunset's alliance with her aunt Morana is stronger than she expected when Omega Sunset begins to criticize Kirakee by blaming her for her problems with Lunar and defending her aunt.

'If you had bothered to spend more time with Lunar, then she might not be this way towards me,' she snaps.

Kirakee protests. 'That's not fair, Omega Sunset. You know I have tried with Lunar. I can't help it if she always dumps me whenever something goes wrong between you and me or me and your father or your aunt. If your father had done the right thing in the first place and supported me instead of your aunt Morana, then you guys would never have been exposed to the wrong way of thinking.'

Omega Sunset is angered. 'Don't speak about people I care about like that,' she snaps.

Kirakee is confused. She frowns. 'What are you talking about? Care about who? Are you talking about your aunt Morana as well?'

'Yes, mother. I care about her too,' she snaps.

Kirakee is hurt and angered. 'After all your aunt has done, you think that it's okay to say that to me. As far as I'm concerned, she has never acted like a normal sister to me. I don't know why you would stick up for her.' Kirakee shakes her head in disbelief.

Omega Sunset begins to walk off. She looks back over her shoulder. 'Forget it, mother. I don't care,' she snaps.

Kirakee decides to look for Lunar but does not reveal what her intentions are for being able to smooth over things between Lunar and her sister, especially since she is not sure how much Lunar might be attached to Morana.

She attempts to gain an alliance with Lunar. With a great deal of caution and a slow and careful process, she openly talks to Lunar about her unwholesome relationship with her sister Morana and tells her why it is not acceptable.

Lunar appears to not be paying much attention while she silently looks forward, gazing over into the valley.

Kirakee finishes off her pet talk with Lunar by saying, 'May the sunset and sunrise be with you and your sister, and the power of the full moon sit with you both so you and your sister will never have a deadly sister relationship like I've had with mine.'

Kirakee begins to move away from Lunar.

As she walks down the hillside, she looks back. Lunar looks back over her shoulder.

Kirakee smiles. 'May the speed of the full moons spirit of peace be with you both.'

Lunar returns a gentle smile.

A Divided Kingdom

Chapter 24

This winter season has been particularly unusual; the snow heavily falls some days and then melts. The same pattern continues every few days. When the snow melts, it gives the pack and Kirakee the chance to go deeper into the forest so they can scavenge for food and clear their boundaries of any harmful threat to the territory.

Stark, Tarkin, and Sheena have been doing very well through the snow season, and Kirakee has made it a daily part of her routine to pitch in with taking care of her big cat friends.

Every few days, Stark spends some nights at Kirakee's new den, and he has built a good standing within the pack. He has helped to grow a lot of camaraderie by sharing his stories.

'I never get tired of hearing your stories Stark. I just hope we will see a better outcome within the kingdom,' smiles Kirakee.

Stark nods. 'We certainly do hope for better things one day.'

Tick Tock flutters over to Kirakee, 'I have some urgent news.'

Kirakee stops her chores and looks up at Tick Tock. 'What is wrong, Tick Tock? Are you okay?'

As he comes to rest next to Kirakee, he says, 'I have a warning. I have overheard Morana and Mud talking, and from what I have gathered, they are conspiring to break up your pack.'

'Gasp! Are you sure, Tick Tock? Why would they be wanting to break up what we have going here?'

'I heard Morana complaining about you and the Legend wolf pack. Apparently, the Legends have spoken to a few wolves about her after the Legends heard the wolves speaking badly about you based on things Morana and Mud have said. Morana has become enraged.'

Kirakee exhales. 'Well, that is of no surprise. Of course, she would get upset, but that's nothing new to me. She has done plenty of that, but when will she ever learn to just quit messing around with my life? So where are they now, Tick Tock?'

'They were on their way to gather the elders of the wolf packs. They are saying you are making all the territory packs look bad because you are caring for their downtrodden. I think there is going to be trouble.'

Kirakee begins walking towards her pack's den. She needs to warn them of the potential trouble.

'Could I please speak to you in private?' she asks one of her strongest members.

They walk outside of the den.

'What's happening, Kirakee?' Hank asks.

Upon her telling him of what she has been told, Hank becomes nervous.

'I don't like the sound of that, Kirakee.'

'I know, Hank, but we have to be brave and stand our ground.'

'What will we need to do, though, Kirakee. Are they coming here to fight us or order us off the land?

'I really am not sure, Hank, but I really believe we shouldn't run away from this because if we were to run, then that would just give them the right to continue running off their slowest or weakest everywhere. It's so wrong. They should be taking care of their own instead of treating them that way,' she says angrily.

Hank warns the others while Kirakee plans to set off on a trip with Tick Tock to see if she can put a stop to the pending attack. Stark offers to accompany them, but Kirakee encourages him to stay with Tarkin and Sheena.

Tick Tock flies above Kirakee as she runs, but he does not know where they are going.

He is surprised when Kirakee informs him they are going to seek out the Legends pack's help.

Kirakee struggles to move fast when they come across a hilly part of the journey covered with thick snow, and she is beginning to grow weary.

As Tick Tock reaches the peak of one of the hilltops before Kirakee, he warns her of what lays ahead.

'Kirakee, stop and hide,' Tick Tock yells out.

Tick Tock flutters back down the hill to Kirakee. He looks stunned. He nervously takes a deep breath.

'Humans. They are over the other side of the hill.'

'Gasp! Humans? What are they doing, Tick Tock?'

'They are sitting around a fire and eating and are surrounded by big machines.'

'Oh, no, Tick Tock. What do we do now?' she nervously pants.

'Stay here, Kirakee, and find somewhere to hide. We can't go any further without being seen, but when the sun goes down, we will have a better chance of passing them in the dark.'

Kirakee and Tick Tock hide in some thick foliage at the base of the hillside.

'Wow, Tick Tock, they don't ever sleep, do they?' she says as they hear the bellowing of voices and machines rumbling throughout the night.

'I think they do sometimes, Kirakee, but if they are still there at daylight, we might just have to find another way to get to the Legends pack.'

They huddle up in the thick of the foliage and eventually fall to sleep.

As the sun begins to rise, Kirakee awakens bright-eyed, and Tick Tock flutters to the top of the hill to investigate and then returns seconds later.

'Sorry to tell you this, but they are still there.'

'Sigh! Okay, we will have to find another way around to reach the Legends pack,' Kirakee says.

Tick Tock begins to flutter away. 'Come on! Follow me,' he calls out.

He flies high above the trees so he can look further around for any other threats, but Kirakee is finding it difficult to keep up with him while running through the forest.

Tick Tock pauses on a treetop. 'Hang on!' he calls out.

'What is it, Tick Tock?'

Tick Tock looks down at Kirakee from high. 'Wait there. I see something up ahead. I'll go and check it out. I'll be back very soon.'

Upon his return, he is panting.

'I think we are too late, Kirakee. The elders are heading towards your pack, and they are moving fast.'

'Gasp! Oh, no, Tick Tock. We must try and get there before them.'

'Sorry to say, Kirakee, but they are way ahead of us, and they are moving too quickly. We will never make it there before them.'

Kirakee looks up at Tick Tock. She sparks up. 'You can get to the pack faster than me, Tick Tock. Stark is there; you can warn him.'

Tick Tock takes flight and flies with speed over the treetops back to Kirakee's pack.

Tick Tock arrives at the den, but he cannot find Stark. He flutters around. 'Hoot! Hoot! Stark, where are you?'

A few minutes later, Stark can be heard as he walks back into the den perimeter. Tick Tock quickly warns Stark, but it is too late as growling, and rustling become louder as the elders enter their zone.

Unprepared, they are now faced with a disastrous situation.

As Kirakee approaches, she can hear a lot of commotion going on. 'Oh no, I'm too late.'

Tick Tock lands on a treetop on the outer border of the den. He is silent for a moment. Tick Tock looks down at Kirakee. 'Brace yourself, Kirakee. It doesn't look very good.'

Kirakee stops for a moment. She looks up at Tick Tock. She takes a deep breath while she is panting. 'Okay, I'm ready, but please if you will, Tick Tock, I need you to get help. Somehow could you please find a way for the Legend pack to know about what is happening?'

Tick Tock does not waste a second. He takes flight and speeds away.

Kirakee runs into the opening of her den's territory to see all her pack scattering and running for the thick of the surrounding forest. Over to one side of the opening, she is shocked to see what is happening.

'Gasp!'

Stark is in a battle with one of the elders, while the other elders are in pursuit of her pack members.

Her mouth drops open as she sees the brutality of the battle Stark is trapped in. The screeching, growling, and snapping are so loud that she can barely hear herself think.

She takes a deep breath and sharply exhales as she musters up the courage to move closer.

As she approaches, a few of the elders notice her presence. They quickly surround her. Before she can say a word, the pack elders are charging forward toward her.

She stops moving and stares silently for a moment as she watches what is coming.

'Stop! Please Stop!' she screams from the top of her lungs with an unusually loud scream.

The battle between Stark and one of the elders suddenly stops. There is an eerie silence while they peer at Kirakee.

'Why are you doing this? We have brought you no harm,' she snaps.

The elder who had been in battle with Stark gets up on his feet and walks over to Kirakee. 'You have brought shame to every pack of every other territory,' he growls.

'How have I brought shame to every other pack of the territories? I have only cared for those whom the rest of you couldn't,' she growls.

The elder moves closer. 'You have made us look bad and weak. You've brought shame to the kingdom of the wolves,' he growls.

Kirakee pleads, 'That's not what I intended to do. No one wants any trouble. I just gave them a home, and for all those who wanted to get stronger again and continue to strive to get well, they have been given a place they can feel they belong too.'

'Well, Kirakee, no longer will this be going on, and we have been looking for Stark because he has been spreading stories about his pack amongst the territories. We don't need his kind in amongst us,' he snaps.

'So, what are you saying? Are you all going to stop me and Stark from what we are doing?'

'Yes. You and Stark are going to be banished from all territories,' he growls.

Kirakee's mouth drops open; she is shocked. 'Gasp! Banished? You can't banish us. That's just not fair. I demand a trial,' she shouts.

'Okay, Kirakee. A trial there will be, but it's just going to be a waste of time,' he smugly says.

Stark walks over to Kirakee. He is closely followed by the rest of the elders. As they walk behind him, they are growling and snapping at him.

'Who will be at the trial?' Stark asks.

The leading elder looks at Stark, moves closer to him, and growls in his face. 'It's a need-to-know basis, and right now, it's not a basic thing you need to know.' The elder turns around and faces the other remaining elders. 'Restrain Kirakee and Stark. We are taking them to trial.'

The elders surround them and move slowly towards them. Stark and Kirakee gradually step backward, but there is no way out of this once the elders are upon them. They cautiously turn around and begin walking with the elder pack in tow.

They are guided back into Morakee. The leading elder instructs the others to gather their own packs to come and attend Kirakee's and Stark's trial down at Orphaned River.

Stark moves over closely to Kirakee. 'What are they planning to do?' Stark whispers.

'I don't know, Stark, but I don't imagine it's going to be helpful,' she whispers.

A few of the elders walk over to Kirakee and Stark. 'Stop your whispering,' one snaps. 'Take them into one of the nearest dens and guard the entrance. They are not to leave,' he instructs.

The Trial

Chapter
25

In one of the dungy dark dens, Stark and Kirakee wait for their fate to come. Sitting in silence, not knowing what to do or say, they sit nervously.

The sun goes down, and they try and sleep but are startled and awoken by every little sound.

Kirakee is cold, so she moves over to Stark and curls up closely to him.

The night has been long, and now the sun is rising. Kirakee and Stark are awoken when they hear Tick Tock calling out.

Kirakee stands to her feet, and in the dimness of the den, she can see Tick Tock near the entrance. 'Tick Tock, what are you doing here. You must leave, or you will be caught,' she whispers.

'Don't worry, Kirakee. They didn't even notice that I came in here.

I want you to know I'm here for you and Stark, and I've told the Legends pack, and they are coming.'

'Sigh! I hope they will get here soon, Tick Tock, because we are running out of time.'

Just outside the entrance, there is some noise, and she can hear a couple of the wolves speaking.

She turns to Stark. 'I think it's time, Stark.'

'I think so too, Kirakee. Be brave.'

'Tick Tock, please hide.'

Tick Tock flutters to the deepest and darkest part of the den.

The leading elder sticks his head inside. 'Come out. We are waiting,' he snaps.

Stark and Kirakee cautiously walk outside the den into the blinding sunlight. They blink until they can clearly see. In front of them are a crowd of wolves, standing and staring at them in silence.

'Gasp!' Kirakee's heart begins to race as she nervously looks on at the crowd.

She cautiously looks around and up at the rock masses, and there, on top of one of the rocks, she sees Morana and Mud looking down from above.

She stares at them for a moment, and just as she begins to look away from Morana, another figure catches her eye. She notices another coming up over the rocks behind Morana.

She looks up once again. 'Gasp!' her heart drops. It is her son Night, and he has now positioned himself standing alongside Morana.

Saddened by what she sees, she hangs her head down.

'*Oh no, not Night too. This day couldn't get any worse,*' she thinks.

She puts her head up again and looks forward. All the wolves in front of her are forming a half-circle before her and Stark. She has never seen so many wolves from different territories gather like this at once. There are at least sixty wolves, but she can't see any of Stark's own kind. She looks at Stark, and he turns his head to look at her. They stare at each other in silence for a moment.

The leading elder walks into the center between the combined packs and Kirakee and Stark. 'You have been charged with bringing shame upon the Kingdom of the wolves. What do you have to say for yourselves?' he shouts out.

Kirakee looks down for a moment and mumbles under her breath. 'Yeah, divided kingdom of the wolves.'

'What did you say?' the elder snaps.

Kirakee takes a deep breath, looks up, and exhales. 'Well, it has been a divided kingdom of the wolves until this moment.'

The elder looks angry. 'Well, one thing we all can agree upon is Justice?' he snaps.

Kirakee looks around at every wolf before her and speaks. 'Justice for what? Shame?' Kirakee snaps. 'What about justice for your own kind not being cared for? Is it an injustice that Stark and I would want to do what others couldn't do by caring? Is there really any shame in that? We haven't brought shame to the kingdom of the wolves. The shame really lays within your own territories.'

'Hush, Kirakee. Don't say any more,' Stark whispers as he nudges her.

The leading elder walks closer to Stark and Kirakee. 'See, this is the kind of defiance we don't need amongst us. You continue to shame us,' he snaps. He turns around and faces the crowd. 'Exile them,' he angrily shouts to the crowd.

The crowd of wolves begin looking around at each other, and there is a great deal of murmuring amongst them.

He shouts out again. 'Exile them. They are to be banished from all territories.'

'Hey, hang on!' says a voice coming closer to the gathering. It is the Legends pack.

'You can't just banish someone because they make you feel uncomfortable,' says the leading Legend.

The crowd of wolves begin murmuring amongst themselves upon hearing what he has said.

The leading elder angrily walks over to the Legend pack. 'Why don't you all return back to your own territory,' he snaps.

The leading Legend lunges forward, facing the elder, 'All territories are ours to oversee,' snaps the Legend, 'and we know Kirakee very well, and we know she and Stark mean no harm, but they only do what they do for the best welfare of all wolves.'

Once again, gasps and murmuring come from the gathered wolves.

The leading Legend turns around to the crowd. 'What have you to say about this. Surely not everyone agrees with the elders?'

One of the gathered wolves walks out of the crowd and approaches. 'I don't see anyone else here disagreeing with the elders.'

Kirakee steps forward. 'My son Alfa Noon isn't here, though. If he agreed with all of what you believe, he would have been here too.'

The leading elder snaps, 'But your son Night is here.' He looks around at the crowd. 'Kirakee's claim isn't sufficient because of her relationship with most of her offspring, and let's not forget about her tainted relationship with Mud and Morana. Kirakee is a troublemaker. Many can testify to that claim.'

The leading Legend turns and faces the crowd. 'Listen here. I declare that this gathering for a trial isn't about Kirakee's personal life status.

Let's not get sidetracked about what the complaint is about.'

Another one of the elders in the crowd steps forward from out of the gathering. 'I suggest the elders' council have a private meeting to discuss a solution.'

Murmuring comes from within the crowd.

The leading elder walks over to the remaining elders of the gathering. 'Who agrees for the elders' council to gather for a private meeting?'

Amongst the crowd gathered, voices of 'yes' and 'agreed' come from within.

Within a few minutes, the elders separate themselves from the gathering and retreat to the same den Stark and Kirakee had been previously imprisoned.

Kirakee looks around, and she sees Morana joining the council. 'Do you see that Stark? Morana is joining in on the meeting as well. What has it got to do with her? Troublemaker.'

Stark shakes his head. 'No good, just not good at all.'

Kirakee and Stark sit outside the den, waiting nervously with the Legends pack while the remainder of the territory wolves sit and chat amongst themselves on the perimeter.

A couple of hours have passed, and in the meantime, the Legends pack do their best to counsel and console Kirakee and Stark.

'We don't agree with the elder's argument, and no matter what, we are always going to be here to support both of you. Be brave and be strong,' the Legend leader says.

The elders emerge from the den. Morana walks back to the same position on top of the rocks with Mud and Night.

The leading elder walks over to Kirakee, Stark, and the Legends pack and faces forward to the crowd. 'Hear me, hear me,' he shouts out.

The crowd murmur and turn around.

'Come closer,' he shouts.

The crowd move in closer to where Kirakee, Stark, the Legends, and the elder leader stand.

Once everyone is closely gathered, they stand silently, waiting for him to speak.

He stands up straight with his chin positioned upright. 'The elders' council have concluded with further assisted evidence that Kirakee and Stark should prove they are capable of showing they care by sending them out to human colonies to rescue any captive wolves, and whoever returns first will not be exiled.'

The crowd gasp and murmur, and the Legend pack are appalled.

'That isn't reasonable,' the Legend leader snaps.

The leading elder turns and responds to what he hears. 'Maybe not for you, but it is for us. Your opinion doesn't lend an option here right now.' he snaps. He turns back around and looks at the crowd. 'Now, all of you, minus the elders, and the Legends, are to escort Kirakee and Stark out of Morakee and send them in the direction of the human colonies. Several of you are to oversee the final arrival and execution of Stark and Kirakee's assigned challenge.'

Chatter and murmurs come from within the crowd.

The leading elder becomes inpatient. 'Stop your chatter and start moving now!' he snaps.

The territory wolves go silent and begin moving around, positioning themselves. They move over to Kirakee and Stark, positioning them in front of the pack, and begin guiding them out of Morakee.

Just as they head towards the borderline of Morakee, Lunar appears and runs over to Kirakee. 'Mother, mother, please don't go. You are in danger,' she cries.

216

Kirakee is surprised to see Lunar. She places her chin on Lunar's head. 'Don't worry. I'll be okay. I've survived many troublesome things before.'

Lunar looks at Kirakee straight into her eyes. She looks incredibly stressed. 'But mother, it's not....'

But Lunar does not get the chance to finish her last sentence before she is interrupted.

'Enough. Come away. Say no more,' one of the elders snaps. He forcefully moves Lunar away from Kirakee. 'Leave now,' he shouts. Kirakee looks back as she watches Lunar being led away. She looks back over her other shoulder to the rocks and can see Morana, Mud, and Night watching. The members of the territory packs shove her to keep moving forward.

One more glance over to where she saw Lunar, she can see the stress and grief on Lunar's face. 'Be strong, my sweet daughter, Lunar.'

Now she begins to be concerned, asking herself whether she will see Lunar ever again. She wonders whether Stark and her will ever succeed.

'*What will happen if I succeed, and Stark doesn't? It won't be right if I return first,*' she thinks.

She looks at Stark while he walks alongside her.

'Hey, Stark.'

Stark continues looking forward. 'I know, Kirakee; I know what you are thinking. Either one of us can succeed, but in doing so, they are influencing an outcome that is to only cause more division.'

Kirakee nods her head. 'Yes. What are we going to do?'

Stark looks at Kirakee and whispers. 'We will have to work out that as we move forward, but for right now, we must make sure we will safely get through this challenge. We need to focus.'

Stark is shoved forward by one of the members of the territories pack.

'Stop your talking, you two,' he snaps.

Kirakee and Stark look at each other, knowing they will need to be silent right now if they are to come up with a plan.

Bravehearts

Chapter 26

The further they travel through the woods; the surroundings are becoming heavily covered with snow. This is beginning to slow them down, and the territories pack members who have been instructed to follow and drive them towards the human colonies are beginning to fall behind.

Kirakee looks back and cannot see them any longer. 'Are they really following us, Stark? They're not doing a good job of it. I can't see them anymore.'

Stark looks back over his shoulder. 'Hmm, it's a bit strange that they've fallen so far behind. There is a possibility, though, that they are holding back for their own safety since we are closing in on the danger zone.'

The day is growing old. They have been traveling for half the day and if they travel any slower the sun will go down before they reach the assigned destination.

Stark stops walking and turns around to see where the territories members are. He exhales. 'Where have they gone?'

Kirakee stops and looks back. She frowns. 'Huh? I don't see anyone at all either. This is strange.'

Stark shakes his head. 'Maybe we should stop here and wait for a while until they catch up?'

Kirakee nods. 'But let's get out of the opening and find some shelter for a while. I'm feeling a bit tired now. You lead the way Stark.'

They begin to walk over to the border of the surrounding forest, but they are suddenly stopped by alarming noises. They can hear loud panting and growling of wolves approaching.

'Gasp! Here they come, Stark.'

They look at the approaching wolves and are shocked by what they see. It is not what they expect.

Running straight towards them is Saber and his rogue pack members.

'Gasp! This can't be right,' says Kirakee.

Evil Saber and his pack are aggressive in their pursuit, growling and snapping.

'You are right, Kirakee. Run!' Stark shouts.

'Run where Stark?'

'Run into the forest Kirakee,' Stark calls out as he runs in the opposite direction from Kirakee.

As Stark crosses the path of Saber, he leaps upon Stark. They begin battling.

Kirakee looks back over her shoulder and then stops. She turns around and gasps. 'Stop Saber, please stop,' she shouts.

Just as Saber's rogue pack are about to pounce on Stark, too, he breaks free.

'Keep running, Kirakee,' Stark shouts.

Kirakee begins running again, but Stark is not running in her direction. Saber and his pack members are completely distracted by Stark and begin chasing him down.

Panting and puffing, she continues running in to the thick of the forest. She no longer can hear or see Stark, Saber, and his rogue pack, but she still does not feel safe.

Confused and rattled by everything that has been happening, she scurries through the forest, frantically looking around while she tries to figure out where she is?

'Psst, Kirakee. Up here.'

She stops and looks around to where the soft voice is coming from. As she looks up, she happily sees one of her forest friends. 'Oh, Tuck, what are you doing here?'

'Tick Tock told me to find you and Stark, but boy oh boy, it's been hard to catch up to you.'

Kirakee is puffing and panting. She takes a deep breath. 'Do you know what is going on?'

'Yes. Tick Tock filled me in. He went to get help.'

'How has he got help, Tuck? We need to help Stark right now.'

Tuck begins to climb down the tree to get closer. 'He....'

Tuck does not finish his sentence because Tick Tock arrives and flutters down onto a tree branch.

'Hoot, Hoot! Follow me. I have a safe place for us to stay for now.'

Kirakee shakes her head. 'No! But what about Stark? He needs help.'

Tick Tock flutters down and lands on the ground next to Kirakee. 'Don't worry. He is going to be okay. I will explain. Just follow me, and I will tell you everything,' he smiles.

Kirakee and Tuck follow Tick Tock as he flutters over the treetops. Once they arrive at a safe place, Tick Tock flies down.

'Stay here,' he says.

He hovers over a fallen tree.

'Stark is alright,' he says.

Kirakee looks down and shakes her head. 'But how can he be Tick Tock. Saber and his rogue pack were upon him,' she sobs.

'But not anymore. Tarkin and Sheena have taken care of that,' he chuckles.

Kirakee looks at Tick Tock. Her eyes open wide. 'Gasp! Tarkin and Sheena. How?'

Tick Tock stares at her in silence for a moment. He takes a deep breath and exhales. 'Well, I better start from the beginning and tell you everything.'

'Tell me what?' Kirakee frowns.

'Okay, Kirakee, but you would be best to sit down because this is a long story,' he frowns.

Tuck starts jumping up and down in excitement. 'Yay! Finally, I get to hear about everything too.'

'Oh, sit down, Tuck, and keep calm,' Tick Tock sounds serious.

Kirakee sits down; she looks intently at Tick Tock with a curious expression.

Tuck snuggles closely to Kirakee. 'Hit us with everything,' Tuck says with a smile.

Tick Tock exhales. 'You and Stark were set up.'

Kirakee gasps. 'Set up? By whom and how?'

Tick Tock stares at Kirakee for a moment. 'This shouldn't be such a surprise, but it was your wicked sister Morana who set you up,' he says with a frown.

Tick Tock explains how he was still in the thick darkness of the den where Kirakee had been held before the trial and before the elders used it for a meeting. With being unable to emerge from the den, he was able to listen in on all said.

Not only does he reveal the things said in the meeting, but he is also able to reveal many things that he has been obligated to keep secret ever since he first met Kirakee.
He reveals that Morana and her aunt have been behind all her problems and trouble, even down to this very day.

Morana has demanded that Kirakee and Stark be put into a dangerous situation. It was her demand that such a challenge take place.

'Your mean sister Morana argued that it wouldn't be fitting to have both of you back in the kingdom, as it would still bring them shame. Therefore, she suggested setting a challenge where it was likely, both of you couldn't return together.'

Upon Tick Tock hearing Morana's plan, he immediately set out to gather Kirakee's pack to oversee the assignment for the sake of having her pack nearby; they could at least help by protecting Kirakee and Stark until they all could return to safety.

However, upon Tick Tock's departure, he was to spot Morana talking to Saber in a concealed location, so then he made it his mission to overhear the conversation.

Morana conspired with Saber for him to gather his rogue pack and cut off the territory wolves that were escorting Kirakee and Stark out of Morakee. Morana instructed Saber to make sure both Kirakee and Stark would never be able to return to Morakee. The plan was for Saber and his pack to destroy both Kirakee and Stark.

Kirakee's jaw drops, and her mouth opens wide. She shakes her head. 'Wicked sister; she is a wicked sister. But why would she do this?'

'That's not the whole of it, Kirakee. There is more,' says Tick Tock. 'What happened next was that Saber went to gather his rogue pack, so I went and gathered your pack, but I knew we needed to do more and plan things better, so I went to see Tarkin and Sheena, and as soon as I told them of what was going on, straight away they went to find you and Stark.'

With every detail, Tick Tock reveals what has unfolded thereafter.

Kirakee's own pack regrouped and came to help, even though their strength is not a complete match against rogue Saber and his pack. But they are stronger than ever before to meet the challenge and have been determined to stop as much of the carnage as they are able to.

Tick Tock explains what happened when they were gaining ground to catch up to Kirakee and Stark and the territory packs.

'Saber and his rogue pack had already been picking off the territory pack members, one by one, by either fighting with them and leaving them wounded or making them scatter in fear of their lives.

'Just as we found where you and Stark were, Saber made his move to eliminate the both of you. We weren't fast enough to stop Saber from attacking Stark, though.'

'As Stark broke free, your own pack arrived. They froze for a moment, and rogue Saber and his pack didn't hesitate to take advantage of the moment. He moved in quickly to attack.

'Your guest pack gathered their nerve, then began charging Saber and his pack, but just as a battle began, Tarkin and Sheena intervened. There was a brief battle between the big cats and the rogue pack, but the big cats overpowered them until Saber and his pack retreated.'

Kirakee and Tuck cheer with excitement.

'That's one heck of an outcome,' she chuckles. 'Imagine that big cats save the day.' She smiles from ear to ear. 'I can't believe it. What a huge surprise that would have been,' she chuckles. 'So, what has come of Saber and his rogue pack now?'

'Well, I didn't see the end results of Saber and his pack being attacked by Tarkin and Sheena. They retreated, but they would still be alive because the plan was to capture them and bring them back to Morakee so Saber and his pack would be evidence of Morana's conspiracy.'

'Wow, Tick Tock, this is amazing.' Kirakee puts her head on Tick Tock's head to express her affection and gratitude.

Kirakee sits up straight again.

'So where are my pack right now. Did they join Tarkin and Sheena?' she asks.

Tick Tock looks sad and stares at Kirakee in silence. He takes another deep breath and exhales. 'I'm sorry to tell you this, but there is bad news; they didn't continue through, and it is bad news to why.'

Kirakee stares at Tick Tock, waiting in anticipation to hear what he will say next. 'Oh, bad news,' she shakes her head. 'What bad news, Tick Tock?'

'I'm so sorry, Kirakee, but we lost half of your pack,' he says with a quivering voice.

'Gasp! What? We lost them. What do you mean?' she whimpers.

'There was a strange and mysterious black smoke. It streamed over the pack. We were all blinded by what was taking place ahead of us, but I knew it was going to be bad because I know what the black smoke is.' Tick Tock hangs his head down in shame.

Kirakee looks confused; she stares at Tick Tock in silence for a moment.

'What is it, Tick Tock? What do you know?'

Tick Tock shakes his head. 'That black smoke was the spirit witch. She took their spirit.'

Kirakee is stunned for a moment. She stares at Tick Tock in silence and then takes a deep breath. 'You mean they're dead?'

Tick Tock puts his head down and nods. 'Yes!'

'No! No! No!' Kirakee cries. She stands up straight and shakes her head. 'I've got to go to them.'

'No! Please don't go yet, Kirakee; it's still not safe. You need to know more.'

'What more, Tick Tock? Whatever more in the world could happen?' Kirakee snaps.

Tick Tock shakes his head. 'Let me explain what I know. Just give me a moment to catch my breath.'

He takes a few deep breaths and moves slightly away from Kirakee like he is avoiding her.

'Tick Tock, you are making me feel more anxious. What is it?' Kirakee sees a curious expression on Tick Tock's face like she has seen a few times before.

'Okay, okay, I will tell you.' He takes another deep breath. 'I believe my mother can answer more questions about what we saw.'

'What do you mean, Tick Tock? How is your mother involved with any of this for her to know how to give us answers? Come to think of it; I've had enough. I don't want to hear anymore.' She snaps.

Before Tick Tock can explain anything else, Kirakee turns around and begins running towards the zone where she last knew Saber was seen.

As she comes out of the border of the forest, ahead of her in the deep snow, she sees several of her remaining pack members standing in the distance. She begins to run towards them, but as she draws closer to approach them, she now can see the remnants of the other half of her pack lying motionless in the snow. She slows her pace and begins to slowly walk over to their lifeless bodies.

She stands over them and stares in shock and then collapses over the stillness of their bodies. She whimpers.

The grief is too much to bear. She stands to her feet, raises her head, and howls like no wolf has ever been heard to howl in all the kingdom of the wolves. The strength and power of her plea for all to stop echoes a rumble through the forests until the trees shake, causing all birds and hidden animals to scatter from all around in confusion.

Tick Tock and Tuck arrive. They want to console her but tremble in fear from the power of her howl. The remaining pack advance with a slow, hesitant pace toward her and the lifeless bodies.

Tuck and Tick Tock quickly retreat into the forest.

She gathers the remaining wolves before her. They are distraught and howl in grief.

'I'm so sorry, my friends. This has happened because of me,' she sadly says.

The strongest of her remaining pack members steps forward. 'It's not your fault Kirakee. We did what any pack should do by showing we care by trying to help, just as you have shown the same to us.'

Kirakee sits and stares in silence, attempting to comprehend his words along with the carnage.

She stands up and recalls the words of her deceased brother Dasher. Words he told her a few times when she was at her lowest. Words she has never applied enough to any of her woes.

'Stand up straight, put your head up, chest out, fight and be stronger.'

She straightens up and faces the pack. A sense of anger is taking over her emotions. 'I have unfinished business I need to take care of, and there must be answers,' she growls. 'But it's not safe here for you. I have lost too many of my Bravehearts, and I don't want to lose anymore. I want you all to leave Morakee and return to our home den territory. Please wait for me there. I'll return when I'm done.'

The pack cooperate and begin running back to their territory, while Kirakee heads back into the forest to find Tick Tock and Tuck.

Secrets Revealed

Chapter
27

K irakee, over here,' Tuck calls.

Kirakee sits before Tuck and Tick Tock. 'Okay, I need answers, and you know more, Tick Tock. Please tell me what you know.'

Tick Tock takes a deep breath. 'Okay, so I told you about today, but I have something else I must tell you now. I'm sorry, but you're not going to be happy about this news either. I hope you won't hold it against me. I hope you will forgive me.'

Kirakee stares at Tick Tock in silence for a moment. She is confused. 'What do you mean, Tick Tock? Forgive you? I don't understand. What is there to forgive,' she says with a frown.

Tick Tock puts his head down and covers his head with his wings. 'I know you are going to get mad with me,' he sobs.

So many thoughts run through her mind. She takes a deep breath and exhales. 'Come on, Tick Tock. Get it over and done with. Surely it can't be so bad?' she frowns.

Tick Tock takes his wings off his head and looks up at Kirakee. 'Okay, I will tell you. In fact, I've wanted to tell you about what I am going to tell you for so very long, but I was forbidden to reveal the truth until this day had come.'

Kirakee shakes her head. 'Huh! Forbidden? This day would come. What does that all mean?' she says with a frown.

Tick Tock flutters over to the fallen tree. He sits down and stares, collecting his thoughts to figure out where he should start.

He clears his throat. 'Well, this story starts back….' He stops and clears his throat again. He has a quiver in his voice. 'This story starts back when you were a pup.'

Tick Tock tells Kirakee her whole life story. Kirakee sobs, growls, and whimpers while she listens to all Tick Tock is revealing. But she cannot bring herself to be angry with Tick Tock. She understands the predicament he has been in and why he has not been able to reveal all he knows to her until now.

Tick Tock flutters again over to Kirakee and puts his wing on her shoulder to console her. 'I'm terribly sorry, Kirakee; I know this must be so upsetting for you to know. I just couldn't tell you about everything because I had to protect my mother. If I'd told you, the spirit witch who claims your name would have destroyed her.'

'I understand, Tick Tock. Now that I know, I can reveal the truth to the elders and then finally put an end to Morana and put Mud in his place for all that he has done too by dishonestly supporting her with all her dirty deeds for his own selfish gain.' Kirakee stands to her feet. 'Come on; we have something big to do. Let's get back to Morakee.

Tuck, you would be best to watch from the trees.'

Tuck sets off before Tick Tock and Kirakee while they stay back and discuss a plan of approach to the elder's council.

'Before we arrive back, we will need to gather the last of my pack and get them to return to Morakee again. They can enter with me while we escort Saber and his pack into the trial arena.'

'Okay, Kirakee. I will go right now and let them know you will be waiting for them on the border of Morakee.'

Kirakee nods. 'Yes! Oh, one more thing. Is Stark meant to be with my pack right now?'

Tick Tock nods. 'I believe so. I'm sure he will be waiting for you with them.'

'Okay, but do you know where Tarkin and Sheena are stationed. Have they returned to their den after they brought Saber and his pack down? I hope they have. I don't want them exposing themselves any further.'

Tick Tock shakes his head. 'I believe they would have returned, especially since they know it is the wish of you and Stark for them to hide.'

'Okay. It's best we do not waste any more time, so let's go,' she says with a frown.

As Kirakee runs back to Morakee through the heavy laid snow, Tick Tock flutters overhead; they chat along the way. He attempts to calm her down.

Kirakee's head is filled with everything Tick Tock has told her. She has so many thoughts running through her head, and she talks to Tick Tock about them. 'So, I wonder how my life would have turned out if all those things hadn't happened?'

'Well, Kirakee, the chances are your life would have been a lot more orderly and less erratic if you hadn't gone through all that you have, but I know for a fact, what you have endured has made you the strong wolf you are today.'

'And I'm glad of that too, Tick Tock. I guess I couldn't have survived without you guys,' she says as she looks up at him. 'But the one thing I've been bothered with and so fed up with hearing is being told to be stronger. I mean, what have they been talking about? I know I've survived because I'm strong, but really? Stronger? I really don't want to ever hear that word again.'

'I hear you, Kirakee, but there is a reason for everything.'

Kirakee looks up at Tick Tock. 'You are so incredibly wise, my friend.'

'I am.' Tick Tock smiles. 'Well, Kirakee, it's time. I must fly on ahead and let them know you are coming.'

Tick Tock takes flight above the trees while Kirakee continues traveling through the thick of the snow. She uses the time to go over how she will tell the elders her story.

'Where should I start? Should I start telling them everything from when I was a pup first and what Morana and my aunt had done from then? Or do I tell them first about what she has done today and then the rest of the story? Hmm, yes, tell them about today first. Yes, that's it. They probably wouldn't even let me finish telling my life story if I started with that first.'

The Tables Turn

Chapter
28

As she approaches the borderline of Morakee, her pack and Stark come running over to her. The rest of her pack have arrived back and have taken over from where Tarkin and Sheena left off and are now guarding injured Saber and his pack.

Stark is so happy and excited to see Kirakee. He begins jumping all over her, dancing around. 'So good to see you are safe and well, Kirakee.'

'Oh Stark, you cannot imagine how happy I am to see how you're safe and well too. I was so worried until Tick Tock informed me of Tarkin and Sheena coming to your rescue.'

Stark chuckles. 'You should have seen the look on Saber and his pack's faces when they saw Tarkin and Sheena. It was gold, and Tarkin and Sheena didn't let them get away, and I mean get away with anything. They got a bit of a hiding from them. Remind me to never mess with cat claws.'

'Yes, I would have liked to have seen that but also to save my friends too,' she sadly says.

Stark puts his head on Kirakee's head to console her. He whispers in her ear. 'Now, you must be stronger and bring honor to their memory. You need to save the Kingdom of the Wolves.'

Kirakee pulls back from Stark and looks at him with a frown.

Stark stares back with a serious expression. 'Yes, Kirakee. You are meant to do this.'

That word again: stronger! She shakes her head.

She understands everything now. She knows Stark understands too. She turns and faces everyone. 'Is everyone ready for what we are about to face?'

She instructs all to follow the plan. They all nod in agreement.

'We have got your back,' one of her pack members says.

Kirakee smiles. 'Thank you, everyone. Be brave. We are about to make history. I think,' she frowns with a curious expression. 'We've got this. It's time for justice.'

There is a subtle cheer amongst them mixed with nervous hesitation. They all turn around and walk into the nearby forest.

As Kirakee walks past Saber and his pack, she stares at Saber. Her stare is fierce and sharp. 'Well, Saber, it looks like your days of being the forest bully are coming to an end.'

Saber snaps. 'You think, Kirakee? My bet is, it's your word against mine. No one is going to believe you,' he smugly says.

'Well, let's see, Saber. Let's just see.'

She takes the lead while her pack members, along with Stark, follow in tow with Saber and his pack.

As she enters the trial arena, most of the territory wolves are lying around, sleeping from exhaustion after being exposed to the

236

outdoor elements all day. Amongst the crowd, she can see many injured wolves licking their wounds, but she cannot see any of the elders or the Legends pack anywhere.

'Gasp! It's Kirakee,' one of the territory's wolves shouts out.

The rest of the wolves awaken from their slumber and stand to their feet. Gasps and murmuring are coming from the members of the crowd as they see Kirakee's pack, Stark, Saber, and his pack, closely following Kirakee.

Upon hearing the noise, the leading elder emerges from the den. 'What is all this noise about?' He looks around and sees it is Kirakee with everyone else. His eyes pop open wide, and his jaw drops. He is lost for words. He stares at Kirakee in silence for a moment before he speaks. 'What is this? Why is it that you and Stark are here with everyone else?' he growls.

While Kirakee walks over to him, the rest of the elders emerge from the den to see what all the commotion is about.

Once Kirakee stands at attention in front of the leading elder, she faces the crowd of the territory wolves. 'I want a new trial, and I want everyone to hear this. Stark and I were set up to fail, and neither of us was ever meant to return. It's not me and Stark that should be on trial, but Morana, Saber, and his rogue pack,' she shouts out.

Gasps and murmuring come from the crowd.

The leading elder becomes enraged. 'Lies, I tell you. She tells lies. Remove her,' he snaps.

Morana makes an appearance. She slowly walks to the edge of the large rock and peers down from above. Mud slowly joins her, and then Night on the other side of Morana. Morana is enraged by what she sees and hears.

'Oh, troublemaker Kirakee has returned, causing more trouble, I see,' she smugly says.

Kirakee turns and looks up towards where Morana is positioned. 'It is you that causes the trouble and lies, Morana. I know what you have done,' she snaps. She faces the elders. 'I'm not saying you have lied, elders. I'm telling everyone Morana has lied. It is her that set Stark and me up to fail the quest. She has deceived us all.'

The Legends pack arrive upon hearing the argument.

'What is going on here?' the leading Legends member asks.

Kirakee turns and faces him. 'Please come over here. I will explain. Everyone needs to hear this.'

The Legend pack begin to walk over to Kirakee, but just as they are within reach of her, Morana angrily leaps forward.

'Remove her, I say. Kirakee and Stark have failed to complete their challenge, and now they are lying so they can excuse their return,' Morana shouts.

Kirakee leaps forward to Morana. 'You are the one who needs to be removed.'

Morana bursts into laughter like an evil-spirited animal. 'You foolish witch's poo. As if anyone will ever want to believe you.' Morana looks straight into the crowd. 'I order you to remove her and Stark right now,' she shouts.

The crowd begin to move forward to Kirakee and her pack, but Kirakee's pack, along with Stark, make a stand and begin to move forward to the crowd. There is a lot of growling and snapping from both sides. They are ready for a battle.

Kirakee leaps in between the two groups. 'Stop! We don't want our fight to be with you. This is what Morana wants. Please listen to me. I tell you the truth,' she shouts.

Both sides come to a standstill. There is silence between both sides. Kirakee pauses in silence for a moment.

'Okay. Please hear me. You need to hear the truth. Morana is guilty on many accounts for the loss of life. This is not just about me.

Please hear me out,' she shouts.

Morana is infuriated at hearing what Kirakee is claiming. She stamps her feet at the rock's edge. 'Cease her, you fools. She is making you all look weak,' Morana snaps.

Mud discretely turns around and slowly walks away until he is out of sight. Night still stands beside Morana, but he now has a confused expression on his face. His glance between Kirakee and Morana is constant.

Now there is no certainty of peace, and everyone is unsettled, so the crowd begin to advance on Kirakee's members once again. There is growling and snapping as they begin to quickly move.

The strength of the crowd is no match for her and her pack's strength. They will surely rip them apart. It's now all doom and gloom.

The Whole Truth
and
Nothing
but
The Truth

Chapter
29

Kirakee's life flashes before her eyes—the sadness, struggles, the betrayal, the lies, the love, happy days, the honor, failure, the evil, her friends, pups, mother, and dreams. Suddenly all begins to come clear. Memories of what she had forgotten, things that were not clear, begin to appear in her memory. She now has a vision of her fall in the Orphaned River, the evil in the black smoke, and the visions she had after the rockfall caused her to become unconscious. The voice, Kira, her words. Clearly and loudly, as if with a scream, she hears them once again, 'Drink the water of the Orphaned River.'

Kirakee gasps. She looks back over her shoulder at the Orphaned River and shouts, 'I've got to drink the water of Orphaned River.'

She turns around and begins to run for the river.

Morana screams, 'Stop her!'

The wolves leap to catch her.

Just as they are upon Kirakee, a loud roar and scream pierce the air. Whimpering and squealing are everywhere. Kirakee looks back over her shoulder and gasps.

Tarkin and Sheena did not return to their den. They had been there all the time, watching and guarding Kirakee and Stark all along while they were concealed in the shrubs.

They have pounced out in front of the wolves, slashing around their paws and claws, creating a barrier between them and Kirakee.

Kirakee continues running towards the river.

The crowd behind is motionless while Tarkin and Sheena hold them at bay. Only the noise of screeching, whimpering, and the roar of Sheena can be heard.

Finally, Kirakee has reached the riverbank. Every noise behind her is like a faint sound in the distance. The flow of the river roars. She pauses for a moment and contemplates what is the truth—drink or not drink. She shakes her head and tries to comprehend her instruction. What to do and what not to do. Time is running out.

'What have I got to lose. It's over now; even if I drink the water and it's wrong, and even if I don't, we are gone. Stronger! Well, here goes nothing,' she whispers.

With two small steps down from the top of the riverbank edge, she is now in reach of the water. She takes a moment to peer into the water and then pops her head down, sniffs the water, and then proceeds to stick out her tongue.

She does one light lap of the water and thinks for a moment, *'It just tastes like normal water.'*

Then without another moment to lose, she begins drinking the water of the Orphaned River.

Everything goes silent. There is no longer the sound of the rushing water, but just a glittering white glow begins to grow. The glow is coming out of the water. Suddenly there is the scent of wild blossoms. Kirakee looks up and around. She is certain there is a presence, and she knows it is her mother.

She gasps. 'Mother!'

But before she can comprehend anymore, she looks back over her shoulder to where the roars, screeching, and whimpering have turned into screams.

With shock and horror, she sights the black smoke hovering over the crowd and her friends. She turns, and for a moment, she stands still and looks on in shock.

A voice comes from within the bright light. It shouts, 'Run, Kirakee. Save them!'

It's her mother's voice, but her voice is mixed with the voice of a human. It almost sounds like her words are echoing.

Kirakee begins to run. The light surrounds Kirakee as she moves. Her pace is powered by the light, and she runs like she has never run before.

She breaks through the cloud of smoke, then suddenly, the light disperses and pierces the black smoke. There is a scream like no other scream ever heard within the kingdom. The light and the smoke fiercely battle. Faces protrude in and out of the smoke, human and wolf. The light and smoke then tumble over the treetops until it all is out of sight.

Everyone begins to stand to their feet. They look around in shock. It is beyond any of their comprehension. For a moment, an eerie silence pursues.

The crowd begin mumbling and murmuring. The silence is broken.

'What was that?' one of the nervous wolves asks.

Kirakee looks around and sees Stark, Tarkin and Sheena and runs over to them. 'Thank goodness, you're alive and safe.' They all give each other a group hug. She then proceeds to the members of her own pack and consoles them. She places her head on each one and gives them words of praise and encouragement.

Just as Kirakee is going to address the whole crowd, a great white owl arrives. She lands on a nearby tree branch next to Tick Tock.

Tick Tock gasps. 'Mother!'

Saber has freed himself and miraculously recovered from his wounds and has now positioned himself on the rock alongside Morana and Night. He looks down at the crowd and stares in silence for a moment. He then looks up and looks straight at Morana. 'It is her, Morana, who made us do everything,' he shouts out.'

Morana begins laughing like a crazy animal. 'You fool, Saber. Do you think you'd be able to get away with trying to pin your crimes on me?' She looks over to the elder's council. 'He lies. Why would I do such a thing? I have no reason,' she smugly says.

Kirakee steps forward and looks up. 'Yes, she does. She has a reason, and I can prove it.'

The leading elder and everyone turn and stare at Morana.

'Do you have anything else you would like to say to defend this claim, Morana?' asks the leading elder.

Kirakee speaks before Morana can say another thing. 'No, she does not. However, I have someone here who can tell you everything and expose Morana for what she really is. Look up into the tree. Tick Tock's mother can tell you everything about Morana, her mother, Saber, and the spirit witch.'

Morana is stunned. She is lost for words.

Kirakee instructs the crowd to listen to the great white owl.

The crowd turn and look up at Tick Tock's mother.

One of the elders' steps forward. He growls. 'Who are you?'

She flutters off the branch and hovers over above the crowd. 'I'm Tick Tock's mother, and I have been the wise owl of the spirit witch.'

The elder wolf growls. 'But why would we listen to you? You are a part of the spirit witch.'

She shakes her head. 'I have not willingly been a part of the spirit witch. I have been enslaved by her and, until now, couldn't speak up because she threatened to take the life of my son, Tick Tock, and to make all my species of owls extinct. But now she is gone and can't touch me. I can now speak up.'

The elder wolf looks around and faces the crowd. 'How are we to trust her. She probably is lying, and how can we believe the spirit Witch has gone?'

Murmuring and mumbling come from within the crowd.

'Why should we trust you?' he growls.

Tick Tock's mother continues. 'Because I can tell you the truth right now and reveal all the secrets from the forest.'

The crowd begins to mumble and murmur again.

'Please let me continue. You need to know it has been Morana, Saber, Morana's mother, and the spirit Witch who have been the cause of all the kingdom's troubles. Not Kirakee.'

The crowd murmurs and mumbles again.

The elder snaps. 'Prove it to us.'

She flutters further over towards Morana. All eyes of the crowd carefully follow every move she makes, but upon laying eyes on Morana, they are to find Saber beginning to quietly sneak away.

Morana begins to back away too; she turns and begins to run, but Night is no longer convinced of her innocence. He runs over and stands in front of Morana.

Morana growls. 'Get out of my way, Night.'

Night growls. 'No, you can't go anywhere.'

Morana becomes frustrated, and she lunges at Night. Within a split second, they begin to battle.

Tarkin and Sheena climb up onto the top of the rock, and the battle ends as quickly as it began. Morana cowards backwards as she is faced with Tarkin and Sheena stopping her in her tracks until she freezes in fear. She does not speak another word.

Meanwhile, while Saber is on the loose upon his escape, Kirakee's daughter Lunar had left Morakee and went straight to get help from Alfa Noon and his pack. When she told him the news of what was happening to their mother, he gathered his pack. Omega Sunset had been staying with Alfa Noon's pack, so she joins the mission. Upon Mist being present, too, he has insisted he lead the pack with Alfa Noon.

With most of Kirakee's pups being together and with the strength of Alfa Noon being known as one of the most powerful Alpha leaders of the kingdom of the wolves, they are a force not to be messed with.

They run towards Morakee with the greatest of power and strength never seen before, while Lunar, Alfa Noon, Mist, and Omega Sunset run in front of the pack.

Lunar spots Saber making a dash towards the woods. She knows he is escaping and tells Alfa Noon.

They change course and head in the direction of Saber.

A battle erupts with Saber, but with the power and force of the pack, Saber succumbs and is rendered motionless.

The great white owl hovers. She looks around to make sure there will be no more interruptions, takes a deep breath, and speaks.

She tells them how Kirakee's mother was an incredibly special and powerful wolf who could make great things happen for the kingdom of the wolves, but she also had sisters who were jealous of her gift in the spiritual realm.

Part of her special gift was being able to shapeshift between being a wolf and a bright healing light, but one day she met Kirakee's father and grew great feelings towards him.

They ended up expecting pups, but because of this, Kirakee's mother was never able to return to being a spirit form again after having her second litter of pups. And because of this, she could not save two of her pups from becoming gravely ill and dying after birth.

She had two sisters and had formerly fallen out with them upon one of Kirakee's sisters being able to shapeshift in the same manner as her; she was what all have come to know as the spirit witch.

Before Kirakee's mother's death, the spirit sister had become extremely jealous of Kirakee's mother because she had favored Kirakee's father first. So, from her extreme jealousy towards her sister and taste for revenge, she drowned her sister in the Orphaned River.

Upon committing her evil crime, she then lost her ability to be able to continuously shapeshift into being a wolf ever again.

Before Kirakee's mother's death, her mother had become good friends with a human woman. She had discovered why the wolves were becoming ill and dying, but upon her discovery, two human men learned of what she had found and attempted to stop her from exposing them. They chased her into the forest while Kirakee's mother attempted to find a place for them to hide from the men.

The wicked Witch took advantage of this moment to destroy both.

The human woman attempted to rescue Kirakee's mother once she was pushed into the river. While they struggled to hold onto each other from the river and riverbank edge, the wicked spirit Witch then pushed the human into the river too. Both ended up drowning in the river together.

Kirakee gasps. She puts her head down and whimpers.

Stark moves over to her and puts his head on her head to comfort her. 'Are you okay, Kirakee? Do you need a break?'

'No, Stark. I need everyone to hear this right now.' She shakes her head.

The wise owl reveals one of many things the spirit Witch was not aware of was, by destroying her sister, she was also to destroy her own ability to shapeshift from a spirit to a wolf. Eventually, her abilities faded away after turning into a wolf a couple of more times.

When she discovered she was limited with her shapeshifting, she captured Tick Tock's mother and made her work for her.

Tick Tock's mother learned about the witches' intentions to ruin Kirakee's life as the offspring of Kirakee's mother, as she suspected Kirakee might have possessed a special gift from her mother to be able to lead the kingdom of the wolves into being much stronger.

Tick Tock's mother tried to warn one of the Legends pack members, but before she could inform him of all the danger, she had to flee upon sensing the return of the spirit Witch. She attempted again to warn him of the dangers, but upon him investigating, the Witch transformed herself into a wolf for the very last time before her abilities to shapeshift completely faded away and deceived the Legends wolf by sending him off into the direction of humans. There he was shot dead.

The attempts of the spirit Witch to destroy Kirakee was also one at the Orphaned River by drowning her like she had done to her own sister.

However, they did know if she drank the water of the Orphaned River, it could possibly cause her mother's powers to be revived, so Kirakee was forbidden to drink the water of the river.

Another thing they never counted on was the fact that Kirakee's mother drowned in the river with a human. Both their spirits combined, creating something more powerful than the spirit Witch had anticipated.

By Kirakee falling into the water after the witches attempt to drown her, Kirakee's partly submerged body was the first thing that activated the beginning of her mother's spirit to be present once more.

When the witch's attempt to drown Kirakee failed, she immediately created Saber and his rogue pack with her powers. He was used to be another way to weaken Kirakee as Kirakee was becoming untouchable.

Gasps and murmurs come from within the crowd. Everyone looks over at Kirakee and stares.

The more the owl tells, the more everyone becomes enraged.

Since the spirit Witch had lost her powers to shapeshift into a wolf, she ended up using the pollutants buried in the land by smothering herself with the toxins, which in turn would help spread the poison throughout the kingdom.

She also used Kirakee's name to lure the wolves who were in search of help from her. Her anger towards her own sister, Kirakee's mother, had her hell-bent on vengeance, and her vengeance has been to destroy everything Kirakee's mother had done to build a strong alliance amongst the wolf packs.

Everyone gasps and then looks to Morana and growls.

Morana steps back and snaps. 'That's not how it was. It's not all true.'

The leading elder snaps at Morana. 'Silent, Morana. You tell lies. You do not speak right now.'

The crowd stare and growls.

Another one of the elders' steps forward and faces the crowd. He shouts, 'Destroy her.'

The Rise Of
A New Kingdom

Chapter
30

Kirakee shouts. 'Stop! Just stop, everyone.'
The crowd freezes and stares at Kirakee.

She takes a deep breath and exhales sharply. 'This isn't the way this should end. There shouldn't be any more destroying anyone.'

The elder walks over to Kirakee. 'Why not Kirakee?' he snaps.

Kirakee faces the crowd. 'Don't you see? You all have been doing what Morana influenced you to do. Destroying each other isn't the solution to making the kingdom of the wolves strong. You all were influenced to destroy me because that's how she wanted you all to be like, just like her. And although your claims against me weren't justified, you all would have destroyed me for it anyway. I

253

never influenced you all to carry on in that way. So why would I accept it right now? I don't, and I won't,' she shouts.

Stark turns and looks at Kirakee. 'Good on you, Kirakee.' He turns back around and faces the crowd. 'She is right, you know. Kirakee has been working to bring us together while all of you only ever wanted to destroy each other. Hear what she is saying,' he shouts.

The crowd stares in silence at Stark for a moment. Then they murmur and chatter amongst themselves.

Kirakee faces the crowd again. 'Please hear what I'm saying.' She pauses for a moment to make sure she has everyone's attention.

'For so long, you all have been influenced to abandon and drive your own kind into harm's way instead of sticking together and looking after your own kind to make sure your own grow stronger and prosper. I have only ever wanted to see this happen as I've felt what it's like to be on the outside, and it only has broken me more. You cannot strengthen or mend a damaged stick if you continue breaking it in many more places.'

The crowd murmur and chatter amongst themselves.

The elder steps forward and faces Kirakee. 'Okay, we hear what you are saying, Kirakee, and I agree with you, but what are we to do about Morana and her mother?'

Kirakee stares at him for a moment while she collects her thoughts.

'I believe everyone should be given a chance to change, and Morana and her mother could be given that opportunity, but in saying that, they shouldn't be allowed to dwell amongst us until they can prove different. Morana and her mother should be exiled. Banished from all territories, and to never be allowed to dwell amongst their own territories until the day they can prove they mean no one any harm.'

Kirakee turns and faces Morana.

'You see, sister, this was never about the kind of leadership you believed you should have or the mean-spirited power you have shown. It has been about justice, right and wrongs. Making things better and bringing our own kind together. This is more than you have done for me or anyone else sister.

Now, I'm sparing your life, but now you will learn to know how it feels to be an outcast, just like you did to me and did to so many others. Live and learn this lesson and learn to be grateful that I gave you good, more than you ever gave me.'

Morana stares at Kirakee in silence for a moment and then hangs her head down in shame.

The elder turns and faces the crowd. 'Remove Morana with her mother. Send them as far away from all territories, for from this day forward, they are banished from the new kingdom of the wolves,' he shouts.

The crowd, Tick Tock, and Tuck cheer. The noise is so loud that Tick Tock's hoots can barely be heard amongst the howls and barks.

The crowd move forward towards Morana while a few of the elders go and capture Morana's mother.

Once together, the pair begin to run from the crowd while the territories packs chase after them, driving them out of Morakee and all other territories.

The elders, the Legends pack, Kirakee, Stark, Sheena, Tarkin, and Kirakee's pack gather to talk.

'So, what happens now, Kirakee, that we have sorted all that out? You make a good leader,' the elder says.

Kirakee shakes her head. 'It wasn't for me all about me being a leader. It has been about me influencing change. Change for the better,' Kirakee smiles.

'Yes. So where do you go from here?' he asks.

Kirakee faces the Legend pack. 'I think we have a job to do?'

They all nod. 'Yes.'

'We can do this. Let's free ourselves of the spirit Witch and her rogue pack from the kingdom of the wolves before the sun goes down,' she says.

Eventually, Kirakee and the Legends pack find the spirit Witch bailed up against what appears to be an old water well once built by humans. The spirit Witch has totally lost her powers and just looks like a smoldering white smoke.

With the help of Alfa Noon, Night, Lunar, Omega Sunset, Mist, the packs, Sheena, Tarkin, and Stark, they all push the spirit Witch into the water well. When she hits the water, a great vacuum goes up into the air and collects Saber and his rogue pack and sucks them down with her into the darkness of the well.

All attending climb up onto a nearby rock mound and heave and push until a rockslide tumbles down over the water well, burying all, making it into an abyss of darkness so the spirit Witch, with her evil wolves, will never be able to be freed and ensuring that is where they will stay for eternity.

Kirakee farewells her mother and her human friend's spirit alongside the Orphaned River. This is the last time her mother will be able to emerge from the water as she used the only power, she had left to help Kirakee rid her evil sister from the kingdom.

Before her mother's spirit begins to fade away, she musters up enough energy to reveal the origin of Kirakee's name to her and tells her about her birth.

It turns out Kirakee's human friend named her when she was born because she was there assisting Kirakee's mother in giving birth. She had the privilege of naming and chose to use a piece of her own daughter's name, Kira, for Kirakee's name because she

256

was the smallest pup born of the litter, smaller than the rest, just like her own daughter Kira. She also reveals where Kirakee's siblings are buried after they passed away.

Once Kirakee's mother returned to the water, only a small sparkling glitter exists to show her mother's and her human friend's spirit resting place.

Nowadays, Kirakee lives with Tarkin, Sheena, and Stark. They share the cave Kirakee had originally made a home for her own pack members since they have moved on and been able to return to their own original territory packs.

Starks Warriors pack has now been accepted by all the other territory packs, so he no longer needs to travel around to tell the story of the Warriors to influence their acceptance but sometimes visits wolf packs in distant territories to tell their young pups the story of Kirakee and the history of all the packs.

Morana and her mother are sometimes seen by other territory packs harassing the human colonies, stirring up trouble for themselves without a care in the world about how that could make life more difficult for themselves.

Kirakee visits the Legends pack frequently to make sure everything is running smoothly with them, and she spends a great deal more time with her own grown pups now.

As for Mud, she was asked what she wanted to happen to him. The elders suggested removing him from the territory. Kirakee declined for the sake of him being the father of her pups but believes that having him in the territory and allowing him to stay by her own admission sets a good example of what she wants others to learn: *don't do unto others as you wouldn't like being done to you.*

Of course, Mud will have to live the rest of his days in the territory with shame, knowing that everyone knows what he had done.

Kirakee, Stark, Tarkin, and Sheena stand on one of their favourite cliff edges and look down into the valley while Tick Tock, Squeak, and Tuck sit high up in the closest tree.

With their view from above, they watch the wolf packs moving through the valley.

As the pack assemble in a row, they have the eldest and weakest walk in front of the pack, leading the way and setting the pace, while the strongest walk slowly behind.

Out on the outskirts of the forest edge, they have a couple of pack members looking out to make sure there are no threats ahead of them.

Finally, the kingdom of the wolves has returned to its oldest ways, taking care of their own kind.

'Look at that, Kirakee. You did it,' Tarkin says with a smile.

'Oh, no, Tarkin. I believe we did it,' she smiles.

They all look back down into the valley and smile. Their hearts are filled with pride.

Kirakee looks up to Tick Tock, Squeak, and Tuck. 'Come on down and sit with us.'

The little critters look at each other with a questioning look on their faces.

'Are you thinking what I'm thinking, Tick Tock and Squeak?' Tuck asks.

The trio shake their heads.

'Yes, but No?' says Tick Tock.

Tuck looks back down to Kirakee. 'Umm, thanks, but no thanks. We are there in spirit,' he nervously says.

Kirakee chuckles. 'Don't worry; they won't eat you.'

Tick Tock shakes his head. 'Nah, we're fine, thanks.'

Tarkin looks up to Tick Tock, Squeak, and Tuck. 'Yeah, we're Fisherterian's,' he chuckles.

Sheena looks at Tarkin. 'Oh yeah, better than Vomiterian's, and that never made any sense,' she says with a frown.

They all chuckle together.

Tarkin looks at Kirakee and smiles. 'In spirit, we are Kirakee's wolf pack.'

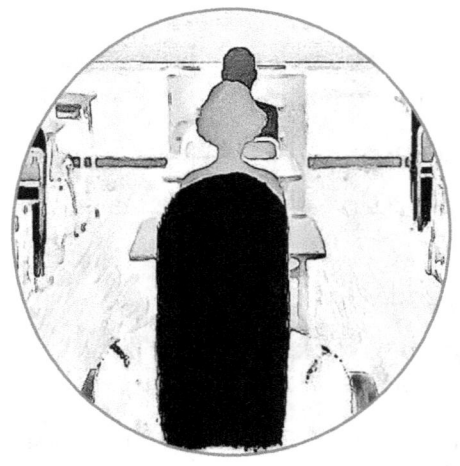

Kira

Chapter 31

A golden pin of light pierces the darkness. There is the faint sound of machines and voices. The pin of light grows until there is a full light of gold. The voices are now loud, and the machines ping with a beat.

A familiar voice shouts, 'I think she is waking up. Get the doctor.'

Her vision begins to clear with the constant blinking of her eyes.

'Kira, you're awake,' her schoolteacher Ms. Time chuckles with excitement.

A few other voices enter the room. 'Please make way!'

The doctor shines a light in each of Kira's eyes. 'Hello, Kira. I'm your attending doctor. I'm so pleased you are back with us.'

Kira constantly blinks as she attempts to comprehend the vision of faces and the surroundings.

'Quickly, we need to remove the intubation and clear her airway,' the doctor says.

Once the airway pipe is removed, she coughs and splutters.

'It's okay, Kira; it's quite normal for this to happen. Just breathe. This feeling will pass,' says a nurse while holding Kira's hand.

Kira looks around the room and sees Ms. Time now standing in the corner of the room, staring intently at her.

'Oh, my goodness, you've come back to us after all of this time,' Ms. Time cries.

Kira attempts to speak, but her first few words are like husky whispers. She coughs.

The nurse gives her a glass of water. She takes a few sips of the water through a straw.

She coughs again, then takes a deep breath. She is frightened and confused. She attempts to speak once again.

Finally, her first set of words come out clearly. 'Where am I?'

'You're in the community hospital. You have been here for quite a long time,' Ms. Time says.

Kira squints her eyes and shakes her head. She attempts to gather her thoughts on whether this is all real.

There is a brief silence in the room.

Kira attempts to sit up in the bed. The sound of the hospital machines becomes louder once again . She looks at the monitors.

She gasps. 'Why am I here? How long have I been here?' Kira sounds and looks stressed.

The doctor leans over and gently places his hand on her shoulder. 'Take a few deep breaths, Kira. This feeling will pass very soon. Just try and relax. We will answer all questions once you are stable.'

She takes a few short and long breaths and sits up further. 'How long have I been here?'

Ms. Time looks at the doctor. 'Do you tell her or do I?' she asks.

'No, I think it would be best for her to be provided with answers from people she knows well.'

Ms. Time takes hold of Kira's hand and gently embraces it with the warmth of her hands. She leans forward and looks Kira in the eyes with an expression of sincerity. 'You have been here in the hospital in a coma for four years, sweet girl.'

Kira shakes her head. 'That can't be possible,' she cries.

'I'm sorry, Kira. I know this news must be coming with a shock,' Ms. Time leans over and hugs Kira.

Kira begins to cry. 'I remember being somewhere else. I saw trees, rivers, lakes, and animals. It all felt so very real; I know what happened to my mother,' she sobs.

'I'm terribly sorry to tell you, my sweet girl, it has been part of your brain dreaming while you were unconscious,' Ms. Time squeezes Kira close to her.

'No, no, no! This cannot be real. I heard mother,' she sobs. 'This being here right now is not real. It cannot be.'

She tries to lift herself off the bed, but she is too weak to move.

The doctor takes hold of her hand. 'I think it would be best for you to rest right now. You've just woken up from a lengthy period of dormancy. It will take you a while to understand everything.'

The nurse puffs up the pillows behind Kira's head.

The doctor requests Ms. Time speaks to him outside of the room. 'She just needs time. It is a big shock to her now, but after a bit of rest, she will begin to settle down. Please come back here tomorrow. She is in good hands. We will be monitoring her very closely for the next 12 hours.'

Since waking up for the past week, Kira has been working hard with the hospital's rehabilitation unit to regain the strength in her muscles and her mobility skills. She is young and strong, and with being aged nineteen, she has made strides in her recovery.

'I'm amazed by your determination, Kira. You are making waves compared to others who have been through what you have,' says her rehabilitation doctor.

'Yes, I aim too. I have four years to make up for,' Kira smiles.

She learns about how Snake, the bully, only known by the name Susan, is no longer a bully but has turned to writing a weekly blog for anti-bullying. She has called the blog 'For Kira.' In fact, her parents are the ones who have been paying for Kira's hospital medical care for the past four years. Susan has been working in her parent's company, and with part of her earnings, she has been paying back the cost of the medical expenses to her parents.

The next step in Kira's rehabilitation is for her to start watching the news on tv so she can catch up on the local and world news.

'Are you feeling up to this now, Kira? There is no need to feel rushed if you're not up to this part yet,' says the nurse.

'I'm ready. Don't worry. The sooner, the better, if this is what it takes for me to get back to living a normal life.'

The nurse leans over to remove a plate of food away from Kira while Kira is sitting up in the hospital bed waiting for the television to be switched on.

'Why are you taking my meal away?' she asks.

'Do you really want me to leave it with you? Watching the news could be a reason to take away your appetite.'

'I think I will handle it. I've seen plenty of nasty stuff in my time. I'm sure I will be okay,' Kira smiles.

The nurse turns on the tv and scrolls through the channels until she reaches a news station that covers the local and world news.

'There you go. You're all set. I'll be out at the nurse's station if you need me.'

The nurse leaves the room. Kira leans over to the side bed lamp and slightly dims the light.

She digs back into her meal and fills up her mouth like a small portion is not good enough. Part of her oversized mouth full falls out of her mouth on to the bed covers. She reaches for a tissue.

She can clearly hear the news reporting. Part of it catches her attention straight away.

'Well, folks, we couldn't even believe this ourselves, but nature can work in mysterious ways.

Recently a field drone was sent out from Bell's Resort construction site to capture some footage for the resorts marketing department, and they captured something most unusual, even considered bizarre.

The footage shows wolves assembling in a particularly unusual fashion by having their elderly and frail wolves lead the way, so they are setting the pace for the pack.

It's almost as if this formation is taking place, so none of the stronger wolves leave their sick and frail behind.'

Kira's mouth gapes wide open. She drops the cutlery out of her hands. The food falls out of her mouth onto her nightgown and bed. She sits motionless.

The news report continues with more footage.

'It certainly is even more unusual for this behavior to be taking place ever since the Bell's construction started four and a half years ago.

Since the beginning of construction, the company has an action plan in place to remove the wolves from the surrounding areas, but as we can see here in the next piece of footage, the wolves are in fact moving around like they are fearless of the nearby construction area.'

Kira gasps. 'It's true,' she whispers. 'It all must have really happened. I know that place. I must have been there. How else would I know that place and know the wolves were already behaving that way before anyone else has now learned.'

She begins to sob. She shakes her head, then looks up and begins to think of what she must do now.

She has a plan. She calls Ms. Time. Ms. Time reluctantly declines Kira's request to drive her to the location, but after negotiating with Ms. Time, she agrees to support her with a set of conditions.

'I will only take you there if you are equipped with pepper spray to protect yourself from bears and wolves, and you must have your GPS active on your phone.'

The Discovery

Chapter
32

Early the next day, they set off to the location. Kira has done her homework overnight and mapped out where she believes she will arrive.

She farewells Ms. Time. 'I will call you as soon as I return to this spot again.'

Kira hitches up her backpack onto her back, full of equipment and food. She bends down and tightens the straps on her shoes.

Filled with anticipation, excitement, and anxiety, she cautiously travels through the dense forest terrain.

A few hours of travel are beginning to wear her down. She is feeling tired. This task feels like the biggest challenge she has ever remembered doing.

She still is not 100% fit and strong for it but her determination to confirm what she believes to be true spurs her on.

Finally, she walks out of the dense forest into a clearing. She gasps. The surrounding beauty is breathtaking. She looks up into the tall trees. She can smell the same scent she has smelt many times in her dreams.

She stops, motionless. She stares ahead with amazement. It is the Orphaned River. The same river she remembers well.

Without any more hesitation, she moves to the edge of the river.

She squats down and begins to sob, but then a peculiar sense of peace rushes over her. She leans over and closely peers into the water. A small glitter suddenly emits from the river.

She gently whispers, 'Mother?'

The glitter grows slightly bigger until it disappears again. She feels a sense of loss, but at the same time, a familiar sense of comfort like her mother used to give her.

She stands to her feet and looks around. A sense of urgency engulfs her, and she has a vision of the Two Moon Lake. She quickly heads towards the location of the lake.

As she draws closer to the lake, the vision of a lone wolf sitting near the edge of the lake causes her to freeze motionless where she stands. She gasps and feels lost at what to do next. The feeling of caution and of a threat is sending her into a moment of fear and sweat.

The wolf turns its head, and suddenly, Kira feels exposed. Not knowing what to do, she takes a step back. Her thoughts are running rampant; her heart is racing. She wonders whether to stand still or turn and run.

The wolf cautiously and slowly walks before her. Kira stands still like a tree.

It is almost like slow motion as the wolf takes another few steps, but as she closes in on Kira, a sense of familiarity takes over. This wolf is the same-looking wolf she has seen in her dreams and visions.

The wolf is now only a few steps away from her.

Kira peers into its eyes and whispers, 'Kirakee?'

Kirakee begins wagging her tail.

Kira puts her hand out for her to smell her hand.

Kirakee's nose touches Kira's hand as she sniffs.

Suddenly, a golden glow begins to encase them.

Everything becomes clear, and their minds connect.

Kirakee looks up into Kira's eyes and says, 'Kira?'

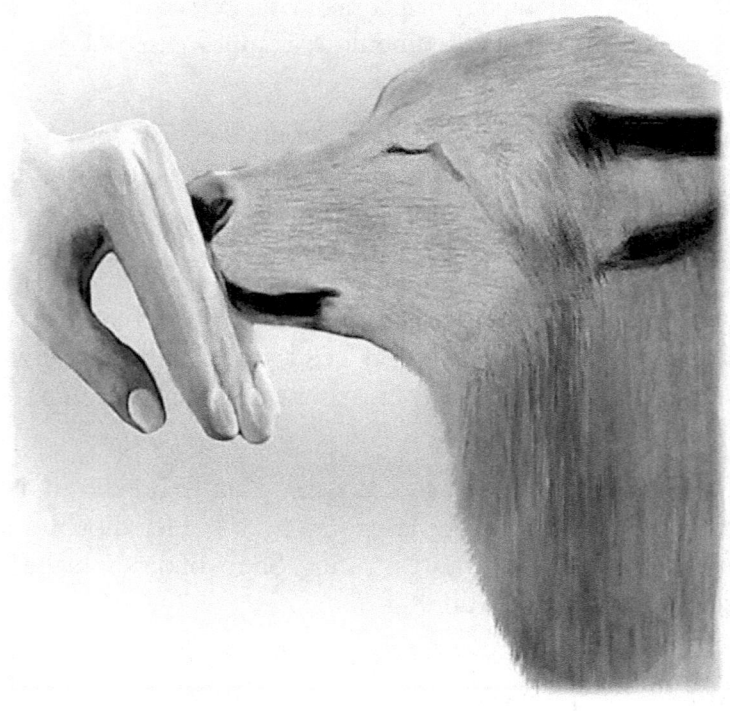

'Yes, Kirakee, it's me, Kira.'

Just like old friends, Kirakee wags her tail and wiggles her back end as she snuggles up close to Kira.

Kira squats down and hugs Kirakee.

Finally, they have met each other, and the dreams and visions are a reality.

Kirakee jumps up and down and licks Kira's face. Kira profusely laughs. They are both filled with excitement and joy.

After an hour of playing and greeting, Kirakee takes Kira over to the lake's edge where she had been sitting. They position themselves with a clear view of the lake.

'This lake is so beautiful, Kirakee,' Kira says with a smile.

'I'm amazed you found me, Kira. For a long time, I thought you were a figure of my imagination until the last days of battle. But thanks to our mothers, they brought us together.'

Kira explains everything that had happened to her, which led to them being able to be connected.

Kirakee shares stories with Kira about how the Kingdom of the wolves are now united because of Kira and their mother's help. But Kirakee has bad news, too, about how the wolves are still becoming ill.

She tells Kira where she thinks she can show her the cause of what is causing the wolves to still be ill.

They plan to travel to the location the next day, and Kirakee suggests a safe place for them to sleep together overnight.

The full moon rises. The reflection of it on the lake illuminates the whole of the surrounding.

Just as it begins to create a twinkling light on the surface of the lake, a faint howl of a wolf begins.

On the surface in the center of the lake is a faint figure sitting and howling upon the reflection of the moon.

Kira gasps. The hairs on her arms stand up with goosebumps.

Kirakee puts her head on Kira's shoulder and then looks at her. 'You, see?'

Kira nods with silence as she looks intently at the figure. She turns and looks at Kirakee in the eyes. Her expression is of confusion.

Kirakee nods. 'It's the spirit of my mother and your mother.'

Kira looks back to the lake. 'But how?' she sobs.

'It's because they became one spirit when they passed away in the Orphaned River at the same time,' Kirakee's voice quivers.

Kira stands to her feet and moves in closer to the lake's edge. 'So, is this why they told you that you couldn't be here after dark because this is what they were hiding from you?'

'Yes! But there is so much more I must tell you, but I will tell you tomorrow because I think you should enjoy this moment of peace.'

Kira sits back down next to Kirakee. 'I feel I should ask, does their spirit show up like this at all in the Orphaned River?'

'No, it doesn't. Only the presence of the power of their resting souls is at the Orphaned River.'

'So, what is happening here?'

'Well, both our mothers lost their lives in the river, so their souls stayed where they died, but their memories moved on into the lake since this is the area my mother gave birth to me and her other pups. This is where our mothers buried the pups, and this is where our mothers grew the greatest bond as friends.'

Kira puts her face in her hand and sobs.

Kirakee licks Kira's face. 'You can be assured; they are at peace. There is no more pain. You can always come here and visit and know they will be here.'

Kira smiles and nods in agreement while she wipes the tears away from her face.

As the hours have passed, the moon has moved out of their sight, and so does their mother's spirit fade. The northern lights are now dominating the skyline.

'This is your favorite thing, isn't it, Kirakee?'

'Yes indeed, but tonight I have another treat, and it is for you. Just wait and see. Don't be afraid.'

Kirakee rises to her feet, lifts her snout up towards the sky, and howls.

A rustling comes from the direction of the lake.

Kira blinks, trying to unravel her vision in the darkness as a mysterious black figure moves alongside the edge of the lake.

She is nervous and becomes restless. She stands to her feet and steps back.

'Don't be afraid, Kira. You are not in danger,' Kirakee says.

Suddenly, out of the darkness, the dark figure appears clearly. It is Tarkin. He cautiously walks toward Kira.

Kira gasps.

'It's okay, Kira; this is Tarkin. He is a black panther.'

Kira looks down at Kirakee and whispers. 'I can see that.' She takes

a step back.

Kirakee wags her tail. 'Come on, you guys, cut it out. Stop scaring each other.' She walks over to Tarkin. 'This is the human girl I told you about, Kira.'

Tarkin relaxes. 'Oh, I see. I thought she was trouble, so I was trying to scare her off.'

Tarkin walks up to Kira and begins going around her while he rubs himself up against her just like a cat.

Kira is stunned.

'Relax, Kira. This is the same Tarkin you have seen in your visions with me.'

'Yes, I know, but I can't believe I'm actually meeting a real black panther right now without being eaten.' She mumbles and stumbles over her words.

Kirakee laughs, 'I know what you mean. I thought the same thing when I met my big cat friends, but he is harmless, and he is a Fisherterian.'

Kira shakes her head and chuckles. She is beginning to feel more relaxed. The joy and excitement of meeting a real black panther in person is taking over from shock and fear.

'May I ask where Sheena is?'

Kirakee looks at Kira after asking Tarkin the question. 'Tarkin says she is sleeping and probably snoring her head off and most likely annoying Stark while he is trying to sleep too.'

Kira squats down to face Tarkin and looks him in the eyes. 'Well, I'm so pleased to meet you, friend.' She rubs him around the neck and ears.

Tarkin rolls his head around in her hands, enjoying all the comforting attention.

With first light the very next day, they set off on their journey to seek answers to why the wolves are still becoming ill.

In the far distance, there is an unusually dark smoldering smoke with a green glow coming from within the surface of the ground.

'That doesn't look healthy to me. Is this what you think is causing the sickness?'

'Yes, I do! I was told the spirit Witch had been smothering herself with something toxic that was found in the environment. I think this might be it.'

'But, if the Witch had been using it as a weapon, and now she no longer exists, then how could this be affecting the wolves. This is peculiar, I must say,' Kira frowns.

She thinks about what this could all mean and has a plan. 'When I go back to where I live, I know someone who I can bring back with me who can look at this,' she smiles.

Feeling hopeful upon hearing this news, Kirakee wags her tail.

After a few hours of spending time with Kirakee and Tarkin, she departs and heads back home.

Ms. Time picks her up and takes Kira straight to the workplace her mother formerly worked. She tells the organization what she suspects she has discovered. They do not ask questions about how or why she found it but are convinced since they had been suspicious after receiving current reports from one of their rescue workers that many wolves had been poisoned by something unusual that does not normally exist in the environment.

Kira leads one of the organization's people to the place where the strange smoke had been seen. She has mapped out a way to access the location without taking anyone through Morakee.

Upon their arrival, they discover rusty old barrels partially exposed on the ground surface, and much further away, they find Kira's mother's backpack partially covered with branches.

Immediately, the report sets off a government investigation.

The Investigation

Chapter
33

A few weeks later, after a thorough and extensive investigation, the government report their actions and findings to Kira and the organization before the information goes public.

The report reveals the barrels have now been removed after finding they were leaking a toxic radiation substance into an underwater steam. This poison was spreading throughout the entire region.

Upon locating the cause of the barrels being placed in the area, they were to find that the previous owner of the land had been paid to bury the barrels on their land. They also found that the former owners of the land had not considered removing the barrels before they sold the land to the company that owns Bell's Resort.

Therefore , by not removing the barrels , they put the company construction workers and the future accommodation clients at significant risk of illness and potentially death.

Their report also reveals that the construction company had taken much longer to build the resort due to their construction company's employees often becoming ill.

The finding also reveals that the company had taken action to remove wolves manually by destroying them because many of the wolves were acting with radical and threatening behaviour in their work area, which seemed to be profound. This finding suggests that the wolves have been affected by the toxin in the environment, and this finding is backed up by the findings of the organization's wolf rescue efforts.

Now, the part Kira has always suspected and although she will find all the answers to complete what really went on that day when her mother disappeared, she pauses for a moment and takes a deep breath.

The findings also reveal that Kira's mother had been investigating why the wolves were becoming ill when she found the barrels. One of the landowners admits after being questioned that he and his father had seen Kira's mother looking around, and the day she discovered the barrels, she was led to the barrels by a wolf.

At first, the father and son were curious as to why they saw a woman roaming around with a wolf on her heels. It set off a few concerns because they assumed the wolf might be hostile.

However, after a long time of observation, they were to learn that Kira's mother had been intentionally led to the barrels by the wolf.

They admit they reacted out of haste to conceal the discovery by approaching Kira's mother and attempted to offer her a payment of silence like they had done before with one of her co-workers.

Upon her refusal, an argument ensued, and they threatened to shoot the wolf as she came out of hiding from a nearby shrub and lunged at them.

Kira's mother threw her backpack at the man holding the gun, and then she ran with the wolf back into the density of the forest.

They then proceeded to hide her backpack and chase her. However, upon their pursuit to catch her, they entered the forest. It was an area they were not familiar with, and something felt off.

Just as they got sight of Kira's mother and the wolf, a peculiar black smoke appeared behind the fleeing two, and it went in pursuit of them.

The men claim they felt fearful, so they retreated out of the forest and removed the barrels, and then buried them in another spot further away.

When no one came looking for anyone or anything, they assumed they had solved their situation by disposing of the barrels in another burial spot.

The report mentioned that Kira's mother's phone GPS was not turned on and suspected she had turned it off because she had attempted to conceal where she was investigating. Therefore, making it difficult for earlier search efforts to find where she may have gone missing.

The two men have now been arrested and charged with multiple criminal accounts.

Kira puts her head down on the desk and cries. 'Stupid, greedy people. You fools!' she shakes her head. She wipes the tears off her face and continues reading.

Upon the findings, the co-worker of Kira's mother was arrested and charged with conspiracy, accessory, and deception. He had taken a payment from the father and son upon discovering the barrels much earlier than Kira's mother.

With the money he received, it enabled him to be comfortable enough to leave the conservation organization and cover all his tracks. He disposed of all evidence of Kira's mother's reports of her suspicions about the area being contaminated, right down to any information she had reported about the Morakee location.

He also admitted that he did happen to drive Kira's mother to her location in his car and drop her off to walk down into Morakee, but shortly after she was meant to return, he received a phone call from the father and son informing him of the events that took place that day. They paid him extra money to keep silent about him driving her to her destination and for him to destroy any other new reports of her work in the area.

Kira stands up, picks up the nearest object, and throws the mug across the room. She puts her hands on her head and sharply runs her fingers through her hair as she screams.

Her body goes limp; her arms fall alongside her. Her knees give out; she crumbles down to the floor and profusely sobs.

Conclusion

One year later, Kira has been enjoying an apprentice role in the conservation organization.

The government has most recently allowed for the Bell's Resort to continue construction since there is no trace of the containment being in the environment.

The news headline reported Kira as the one who unraveled the mystery of her mother's disappearance, and since then, they have offered to pay her money for interviews on their talkback shows, newspapers, and magazines. Kira has chosen to remain silent for the sake of not revealing Morakee.

Kira's aunt never returned from a new overseas trip she took after one year of Kira being in a coma. Only after Kira's awakening from the coma had she bothered to FaceTime Kira a couple of times.

The government cordoned off the forest. Since then, the entire area of Morakee and up to a one-hundred-kilometer radius has been declared a wolf sanctuary because Bell's Resort and the government decided they owed the wolves protection since they were one of the key reasons why the contamination of the environment was discovered.

The government and Bell's Resort gave Kirakee the job of naming the sanctuary, and she named it, *Our Mother's Wolf Sanctuary.*

Kira learned there had been a pair of backpackers who had entered Morakee by accident after becoming lost in the very early years of Tarkin's and Sheena's presence. Upon them seeing Sheena, it set off an extensive search. Hunters in their search had stumbled upon Morakee, too, but after they had started to eliminate wolves in the area since they considered them a threat, they decided to leave and never return to the area as they deemed it to be too unsafe.

The government offered to search for Kira's mother's remains, but she has requested her mother be left to rest since she had found evidence of her mother drowning in a river where the wolves reside, and that is where she knows her mother would rather be left in peace.

Often, Kira visits Kirakee and her friends. She spends many hours sitting down by the Two Moon Lake and looking out over the valleys with Kirakee and Tarkin.

She finally met Stark, Sheena, Tick Tock, Tuck, and Squeak. They all have accepted Kira as being like a human version of Kirakee.

After a lengthy search, she also found Tarkin and Sheena's master. He came to take the big cat's home, and they were extremely happy to see him, but they chose to stay in Morakee with Kirakee instead of returning home with their master.

During the snowy winters, their master returns with food to help them out, but even after Kira informed him of the cats' new diet, he discovered his beloved big cats expressed their preference by snubbing anything other than fish with a big feline hiss.

A year after all things were revealed, an author contacted Kira and told her she had a little robot dog who was like a drone enter Morakee. The mechanical dog had encountered Kirakee when she was still a pup. However, a couple of years later, the robot dog returned to Morakee and recorded Kirakee's story. The footage is clear enough for her to write a story about it all.

She asks Kira if it would be okay for her to make a book with Kirakee's story and have her contribute her side of the story to the book. Kira gave permission and collaborated with the author. The book was released shortly after as a fiction story, and it has been called, *Kirakee's Wolf Pack (Howl Upon the Moon)*.

Every time Kira visits Morakee to see her friends, she becomes like one of the packs.

Kira, Kirakee, Tarkin, Sheena, and Stark together roam the forests, and while doing so, some of the adjoining territory wolf pack members discretely stick their heads out of the forest tree line to peek at them running through the valleys.

'There goes Kirakee with a few of her really messed up looking wolf friends,' a wolf whispers.

'Yeah, really, really messed up looking wolves,' another shakes his head.

Then the wolves quietly turn around and run back into the density of the forest for fear of being seen by these strange-looking animals they have seen around with Kirakee countless times.

Days are never filled with loneliness like Kira and Kirakee had encountered in their earlier days before they knew each other and their friends. Now they run through the forest with their big friends and embrace every happy moment while feeling the warmth of their mothers' spirits while they imagine them running free with them as one big magical and happy family.

ACKNOWLEDGEMENT

I would like to pay tribute to the following people who gave their support, and encouragement to help me finally come full circle in my artist journey so I could finally publish as a novel, Kirakee's Wolf Pack (Howl Upon the Moon)

First off, I must thank Ron Van Peelen for the support he gave me at the start and throughout my artistic journey. By helping me prepare my illustrations with my synopsis of Kirakee's story and snippets of the scenes to sell with the illustrations through his artisan shop, this inspired me to grow as an artist.

Ron was an extraordinary mentor, and incredibly good friend to me and to many of the Tasmanian artists. He was also a passionate artist and business owner of The Tasmanian Artisan Shop https://www.ttas.biz/

His insight, humour, intelligence, and honesty guided me to be where I am today. He is sadly missed.

A very special thank you to a few of my fellow authors and creatives on social media for the love, laughs, inspiration, and friendship. Nisha, Raffaella, Cindy, Jules, Han, Malavika, Ellen, Vishal, Dominique, Paula, and many others who have been my wolf pack Alpha's.

Also, a special thanks to all my other Instagram followers and Facebook friends. Thanks so much for the encouragement, support, love, and friendship.

Through rough drafts, busy work schedules, a world of change over the past few years, thank you to my wonderful daughter Loren for always being my sounding board for my storytelling.

To all my kids, Nathan, Josh, Loren, and Isabelle, thank you for the love and encouragement.

ABOUT THE AUTHOR

The author, artist K.C. Morcom, is a former magazine writer and publisher.

Her earliest and current book publishing have been inspired by social and personal topics. In each book topic she addresses key issues to inspire change, whether that be to do with nature or the human spirit.

The books reflect her magazine publishing style by the fact she not only makes a book entertaining, but she also creates the books to have multiple layers of interest so as to inspire and educate.

All her book titles are fully illustrated, fiction or non-fiction.

She is an artist, author, illustrator, and storyteller.

Since becoming an author, most of her books have been created for various causes. She is a long-term charity support worker.

KC is a lover of nature and a huge fan of our bird species and honeybees.

Most of her artwork involve images of birds, cats, dogs, koala's, butterflies, wolves, bears, raccoons, squirrels, honeybees, and sunsets.

She has created several books during her artistic journey and Kirakee's Wolf Pack (Howl Upon the Moon) celebrates her journey for coming full circle, in turn this has enabled her to finally publish the story into a complete novel for the very first time since being copyrighted 2018 and previously published in short with illustrations.

BOOKS BY THIS AUTHOR

Non-fiction

The Bird Whispers and the Bird Whisperer brings about awareness for our need to protect nature.

Fully illustrated, multi layered with short rhyming stories.

Part two of the book has bird watching tips, everything you need to know about birds and cats with comprehensive bird and cat profiles. The book also includes an art medium index for art lovers and is suitable for all reading age children and the family. Available in Gloss Hardcover 8 x 8-inch, Paperback, and Part 1 eBook.

Non-fiction

The Bees, the Bag, and the Artist. A fully illustrated, educational book with a short story. Part two, has everything you need to know about honeybees. This book has an underlying theme for compassion causes and is suitable for all reading age children and families.

Available in Gloss Hardcover 8 x 8 inch.

Fiction

Missy Boo and Moochiepoo

Fully illustrated children's book with a short rhyming story about the friendship and adventures of a cat and dog.

Available in Gloss Hardcover 8 x 8 inch.

BOOKS BY THIS AUTHOR

Non-fiction
A Gentle Reminder (Sunsets, Sunrises and Rainbows) is a sentiment booklet. Fully illustrated. The photography accompanies a poem. The poem consists of several key prompts to help a person to refocus and look forward when they are going through a challenging time. Laminated Gloss Paperback cover, 5 x 5 inch.

Fiction
Mystery/Fantasy
Kirakee's Wolf Pack
(Howl Upon the Moon)
KC Morcom's debut novel.
Fully illustrated.
This story has an anti-bullying theme.
Available as, Gloss Paperback, 6 x 9 inch. Gloss Hardcover, 8 x 8 inch, and eBook.

A WISE OLD FRIEND

A wise young owl flew down from a smoking tree.
His mission was to oversee our story protagonist, 'Kirakee.'

Secrets were sealed, and there was news that
could not be revealed.

Loyal and wise, he watched a development evolve
before his very eyes.

He spoke when he should, but listened more, and done
what he could when, he was sure.

A rare friendship he gave, a life he would save.

A kingdom would fall and rise again.

Standing together at the end, were a
group of unique friends.

By
KC Morcom

THE HOPE FOR BETTER THINGS TO COME

You should never give up.

No matter how hard the situation is.
Always believe that something beautiful
is going to happen.

Hope for change.

Hope for better things to come.

Eventually, things do get better.
That golden day will certainly come.

But with giving up, you will never know.
So, allow your curiosity, to flow.

KC Morcom/KCM Inspirations, Designs & Products

Redbubble, KCM Inspirations,
KCMinspirations.redbubble.com

TeePublic, KCM Gems n Bling
KCM-Gems-n-Bling@TeePublic.com

www.ingramcontent.com/pod-product-compliance
Lightning Source LLC
Chambersburg PA
CBHW061923130726
47909CB00012B/575